RUNAWAY BRIDE

7 Brides for 7 Bears

MOXIE NORTH

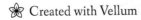

PROLOGUE

"Ida, don't you have any of those taffy candies? The caramel ones I like?" Velma asked, bent over looking in a low cupboard in Ida's kitchen. A long, striped tiger tail came out from under her skirt. It lay limp, dragging on the floor.

"I don't understand why you're askin'. You can't have them with your dentures anyway!" Ida called out from another room. "And tuck your damn tail away. Why can't you control that?"

"I do not have dentures and you know it! No Kindred lose their teeth, can you imagine? Your clan would be hilarious with a bunch of gummy bears wandering around," Velma scoffed. "Stop picking on me about my tail. Half the time I forget it's out and I don't have the energy to make it go away."

"You said gummy bears," Mary cackled from the kitchen table.

"Mary, just because you're the youngest, doesn't mean you get to give me sass," Ida said, shaking her finger as she walked back into the kitchen.

"I'm sixty-three, you call that young?" Ethel asked. "And you want to talk about sass? Did you put your makeup on when you were shifted this morning? It looks like your eyebrows are kissing your hairline. It's just terrible."

"Please, you probably still only occasionally need naps. I would die without them," Velma said dramatically. "Stop teasing Ida, those wolf eyes of hers aren't what they use to be."

The little kitchen was decorated with retro appliances, all in matching teal colors and geometric designs that people now found trendy. However, this wasn't just a trendy kitchen with a retro vibe, these items were original, well used, and well cared for. Right down to the formica countertops and vinyl upholstered chairs. The scene was set with the four women that were puttering around in it. But they weren't gathered for an afternoon bridge game, it was for something much more important that had brought them together in Ida's kitchen today.

"Always so dramatic!" This came from Fannie

who had been in the bathroom and had heard their entire conversation.

"You know this isn't really a gathering if everyone isn't here," Mary told the group as if they didn't already know.

"We'll Skype them, it's not hard," Velma said confidently.

"I hate that thing. I look terrible on it. If the Great Mother wanted us to be digital she would have given us screens for faces," Fannie said taking a seat. Reaching into an oversized bag, she pulled out a giant Rolodex. "This has worked just fine for me for years."

Mary started to laugh. "Welcome to the twenti-eth-century ladies. Fannie, can I teach you about spreadsheets? It's not like they haven't been around long enough for you to give them a try."

"I need to feel the paper. It's my thing, don't question it," Fannie huffed.

The ladies arranged themselves around the round table. Velma flipped open the lid of her Rolodex while Mary sighed and placed her laptop on the table. Velma got up as if she'd been reminded and opened a drawer to retrieve a laptop that looked as though it weighed triple what Mary's did.

"Gimme a sec. Gotta make the pictures work."

The woman organized and jockeyed for space on the table while the video call rang through. It picked up and two elderly women's faces appeared.

"Betty, Ruth, can you hear me?" Velma yelled to the screen.

"Yes, stop yelling, Velma. Can we get this started? I have a pie in the oven," Ruth said with a sigh.

"Well, excuse me; I thought this was a sacred gathering of the Crones. I didn't know it was an inconvenience to everyone's schedule." Fannie said waving her hand in the air.

"There just has to be a faster way to do this. Let's cut to the chase. Has anyone gotten anything?"

The woman looked to each other to see who was going to start.

"I don't currently have anything," Betty started over the screen, her voice in slight delay to her movements. "I think I'm getting a new apprentice. I've been dreaming about a young woman from the Dagaz Clan."

Fannie made a coughing noise. "Don't you think I'd have been given a Post-it note or flying bird to notify me if one of my clan was going to be heading your way?"

"Maybe the Great Mother lost your number?"

Betty said with enough cattiness that a few of the woman gasped, the others laughed.

"Frigga talks to me all the time!" Fannie said indignantly.

Velma threw a cookie across the table at Fannie. "Really? You're on a first name basis?"

Ruth cleared her throat before starting. "Ladies, we are Crones chosen by the Great Mother, Frigg, Gaia, whatever name you may choose. She also speaks to us all in different ways. Let's respect our individual gifts and move on." She said these words with finality. Ruth was over a hundred and seven years old and no one wanted to get on her bad side. Her link to the force that created their world could not be disputed.

"Yeah, Velma," Fannie said under breath.

Another cookie flew through the air.

Mary finally spoke up to stop the food fight. "I'm not sure if I got anything. My signs haven't lined up as I expected them to."

"You need to stop looking for signs! You need to feel it!" Fannie exclaimed.

"I like my signs, shut up about them," Mary ground out. "The signs just have to be read. I saw a group of starlings flying overhead in a broken V yesterday."

"And that means?" Ida inquired.

"I'm not sure yet, but I know it was a sign!"

Ida threw up her hands in frustration. "Can we get back to business?"

"I think there is someone coming, but she hasn't been found yet. I think it's one of your boys, Ida," Betty said, flipping through the little notecards that she spun with precision. "I have their names here somewhere."

"I'd like to see you call them boys to their faces. The men of King Security International wouldn't like being called boys," Ida said.

"I'll call them whatever I want, the whippersnappers. That's beside the point; I've seen one of his men a few times in my dreams. It must mean something. It's a tall fellow, dark hair, muscles, lots of 'em," Betty said, looking down at the screen like she was reading from her notes.

"Oh well, that's helpful, Betty. Have you seen the brick houses that work for KSI? They're all tall, dark, and handsome. Even the blond ones," Ida said with annoyance as she spun through her cards.

"Let's see... King? Couldn't be their intrepid leader. That man is a grump and I doubt we'll ever find him a mate. What about Zion?" Ida asked.

"Zion, no, I remember his face. The one I

dreamed about had a face that was thick, broad," Betty explained.

"How in the world do you call someone's face thick?" Mary laughed. "Pockmarked, rugged, hell, even ugly. That's how you can describe someone."

"It's strong is what I mean. He frowns, at least he did in my dream and he has a tattoo on his upper bicep. An eagle and a flag or banner, also something about corp, something like that."

"Well, that has to be Van. My notes say that he was military. That would explain it," Ida said happily. "What else do you know?"

"Just that he needs to travel to find his mate. She's missing? Lost? Or maybe she's just hidden. I can't tell exactly. I just know that he needs to be the one to find her," Betty said confidently.

Mary gave a deep sigh and said, "Shouldn't the Great Mother give us a little more to go on? Always this puzzle."

"Love is a puzzle, my dear, it's never cut and dry. And with our Kindred that mating call can be elusive. You never know when it will hit or why. Our job is to make sure our kind continues, and that means making sure that the right humans are mated with our available ones and our bound heart Kindred find the shifter mates meant for them." Fannie had been sitting back with a pile of yellow yarn in her lap that she was just starting to knit and purl.

"Fine, but it doesn't mean that a little direction would hurt," Mary harrumphed.

"I'll arrange a meeting with King. Next on the list?"

CHAPTER 1

"Hello? Anyone? Someone? Smelly rude man?"

Cora Butler was cold, wet, dirty, and pissed the hell off.

Raising her voice to a shrill screech, she tried again, "Hell-fucking-O! I have to go to the bathroom! I don't *want* to because that nasty toxic toilet that has never seen bleach is not my idea of a good time, but I have to go!"

She'd started screaming about fifteen minutes ago when she only slightly had to go. Knowing that her captors were not going to be rushing to her aid, she figured that she had better start early.

There were two men, judging by their general smell and appearance, that were keeping her in the room she had not exactly grown accustomed to over the past few days, but certainly had thoroughly examined.

Frick and Frack, as she had decided to name them, had kidnapped her from a perfectly acceptable cheap motel where she had been eating a bucket of chicken and watching the shopping channel in the wedding dress she had been trying on when she decided to run.

Run. She'd wanted to get away, and she did. She desperately needed a break. A break from the monotony of her life, from the emotional void that she had slipped into with very little resistance. Cora needed time to gather her courage and her strength and more importantly, to plan out what she was going to do with the rest of her life. She wanted a fresh start, that much was clear. It wasn't going to be easy, and there was a good chance she'd have to move back to Texas to stay with her parents. Ugh. But it might just be worth it.

But that would mean getting out of the very specific mess she was in right now.

Sure, there was a chance that the authorities were looking for her, especially since the gown wasn't fully paid for when she'd run off in it. But there was also a very hefty deposit on it, and if they wanted to charge her fiancé's credit card the additional ten thousand dollars, he'd pay for it.

Thinking back on it now, a more detailed plan on where she was going and what she was going to do when she got there should have been involved in her getaway. Possibly a little insight that she might not want to be sitting around in a questionable hotel on a comforter that was clearly overused in a dress worth the same amount of money as a decent car.

When she had tried on that dress it was the first time in years that she had felt beautiful, even happy. Chaz had told her to buy what she wanted. Just like he'd told her to hire a wedding planner and do whatever she liked with the ceremony. It was almost a theme for their relationship, when he'd proposed, he told her to pick out a ring in a magazine and he'd get it for her. Transactions. That's all these special moments were to him.

In his limited defense, Cora had never complained. She never asked him to give her more time, more attention, and that was on her. The dissatisfaction had crept up on her, and maybe it was easy to ignore for so long because she found her happiness in other places. Living the life she did gave her so many opportunities. She had worked with so many great people, and developed skills that she could be proud of. So when plans got canceled or Chaz was distracted, even when they were together, she looked past it. There would always be more plans, more dinners, and more parties to attend.

Cora had spent over four years with him. From their junior year in college to a few days ago, she'd done her time. She'd followed him through school, attended the dances, the balls, and charity functions his family required. The first year they'd spent together as a couple had been amazing. It had been fun and exciting; almost perfect.

Over the next few years he had gotten busier with work. She supported him, and knew that it was important for him to establish himself in the business world. It wasn't until after the engagement, that she started to feel they were more like roommates. But she was there, doing her part and being a supportive partner. She learned how to play tennis, make scintillating small talk, and how to drink just enough at all of those charity events to keep a happy glowing buzz about herself so that she didn't have to think about how boring and pointless it all was.

Cora wasn't surprised when Chaz asked her to marry him either. In fact, she'd stopped being surprised at anything he did after he had introduced himself as Charles and then she found out that was his father's name and everyone called him Chaz instead. Cora would have dumped him on the spot for the name alone. But he was handsome, well connected, and he treated her well. There wasn't anything to complain about. Who passed up a successful handsome man because of a cringe-inducing name?

"I'm going to hold it until I get a urinary tract infection that will go septic and kill me! How much money do you think you'll get for me then?" she screamed into the silence.

Three days ago Frick and Frack had put her in a boiler room that was straight out of a horror movie. They had tied her hands behind her back with rope and Cora was pretty sure that her shoulders would never recover. The state of her feet were disgusting. Frick and Frick hadn't considered her need for footwear during her kidnapping, leaving her with filthy bare feet. Walking across the dirty warehouse floor made her feel even grosser. They only unlocked her so she could go to the bathroom and that was twice a day if she was lucky. Not that they were feeding her or giving her enough water to make that much of a challenge.

She was too angry to get sick. Sure, she was cold and damp and there was a constant drip in the room from a number of pipes.

The odds of her peeing her expensive wedding dress weren't high, but there was some small comfort in screaming at those morons. She'd like to think that if she hadn't been encumbered by hundreds of yards of tulle and the enormous bucket of chicken between her legs, she could have fought off the attackers that burst through her door.

The only thing that was really pissing her off was that it had been three days, and nobody had come for her. Add that to the two days she'd been hanging out in the hotel room and eating her way out of that dress, and either nobody was looking for her, or Chaz was doing a cost analysis on whether she was worth it.

Chaz didn't love her.

Cora didn't have an emotional response to that realization. It definitely wasn't new. She'd realized that a few years after college. They'd been on a trip to Turks and Caicos. Three days into their trip she had been lying on a lounge chair, her white bikini hugging her curves, and an icy blended drink in her hand while Chaz stared at his phone, his face anything but relaxed.

She'd wanted him to put the phone down. To look up and see the crystal blue water and white sand beach. They were in paradise together and he was working.

"Do you want to go inside?"

"No, babe, this is fine."

"A drink? I can get you one?"

"Babe, I'm working."

"How about a massage? I can schedule you one?"

He finally looked up from his phone. "Seriously, babe, why don't you go shopping or something?"

It was at that precise moment that Cora realized she couldn't remember the last time he had used her name.

Babe. It was like saying 'Pal' or 'Buddy' when you couldn't remember someone's name. Did he remember her name? He never said 'babe' with any kind of affection either. He used it like it was her name. In fact, he used a lot of annoying endearments, but rarely called her by her name.

That was the first time she noticed that Chaz didn't really see her. Not as any kind of partner, that was for damn sure. She was an accessory.

Her feelings of hopelessness had built steadily from that point onward, until that day in the bridal salon. Standing in front of a wall of mirrors, all of them angled to point directly at her, she'd paused. She'd paused a little too long because it gave her time to think. Cora asked the bridal consultant to give her a moment. As soon as the woman left, Cora looked at herself. She really looked, and saw the dark circles under eyes. The pale skin. The disappointment. She didn't look like a bride. Her mother hadn't been able to be there with her and she didn't really have friends anymore. She was all alone. And it dawned on her that she wasn't just alone in the salon. She was alone every day.

Cora looked at her dress with someone else's eyes. It was beautiful. A full ball gown with tulle and lace skirt and a fitted bodice with a plunging sweetheart neckline that revealed her cleavage. This dress deserved to have a happy bride. One that was surrounded by friends and family oohing and ahhing over it. Not a woman checking it off a list.

Cora proceeded to have the mother of all panic attacks, and then she ran. Literally ran for her life in a fifteen thousand dollar wedding dress.

Originally, she had planned to spend a few days in a hotel rethinking her life, and then she'd go back and break up with Chaz and get the hell on with it. Then Frick and Frack had stepped in, and everything had turned to shit.

Oh, the shame of letting those bumbling idiots get the best of her. They were stupid. *Really* stupid. They fought constantly with each other. Cora laughed out loud when they realized on the second day neither of them had sent the ransom request.

They would yell, and then whisper amongst themselves. It would have been comical if she wasn't in a wet dress, starving, and in need of a toilet!

The rusted metal door across from her swung open and Frick walked through. He was wearing the same clothes he'd had on for the last three days, and she could smell him across the room.

"Finally! Seriously, you guys are the *worst* kidnappers. I mean you could have kept me anywhere and you pick this ridiculous horror show room? Are you really that bad at hiding?"

"Bitch, nobody asked you!"

"Of course not, and I didn't get asked to be kidnapped either, moron. Now let me up to pee."

"Didn't you just go?"

"That was yesterday, you rocket scientist. Just like it was yesterday the last time you gave me any water!"

Cora could have found this funny if she wasn't feeling the pain in her joints and a disturbing realization that there might not be a light at the end of this tunnel. She had fully expected Chaz to have her out of there in twenty-four hours, but that hope had been dashed when Frick and Frack failed Kidnapping 101 and forgotten to follow through with telling anyone they had her.

"And by the way? Did you *really* send the ransom request this time? I'm not trying to tell you how to do your job, but really, this is getting old."

"We sent it," he said with a sneer, his yellow teeth flashing.

"And?"

Frick's sneer turned uncomfortable. He licked his lips and his eyes darted away from hers.

"Well?"

"We haven't heard nuthin' yet."

"What the hell do you mean? Please tell me that you sent it to the right person. My fiancé is Charles Dillard the Third. Better known as Chaz. He works at the Dillard Building in downtown Seattle. Not hard to find. It's tall, shiny, and says Dillard on the side?"

"We sent it and we got nuthin'! Maybe he don't want you. Ever think of that?"

Clearly, Frick was trying to make her feel like this was some kind of failure on her part. *As if*.

"I think that my fiancé sees me as an investment and Chaz Dillard never lets go of an investment."

Cora was reluctant to admit it, but that investment was one thing that was giving her hope. Chaz had invested time and money in her. He wasn't going to lose out just because of a minor hiccup like a kidnapping.

At least she truly hoped that was the case. The brief time she had spent reviewing her life had led her to believe that she wasn't going to be breaking any hearts when she split up with Chaz. He'd be mad, but it wasn't as though he would be losing the love of his life. Not by a long shot.

Telling those morons that her fiancé would pay for her safe return sounded as hollow to her ears as it felt in her heart.

CHAPTER 2

"Luca, do you have eyes on the target?"

"That depends, was there another reason I've been laying on this rooftop for over an hour?"

Van didn't question the man with his eye to the sight of a sniper rifle. Van's assignment was to follow their client as he made his stops for the day. They had moved between three different diamond exchanges, each one was in a nondescript building, and this should have been a routine job. But their client was nervous, and rightfully so. He had been trapped by a group of highly trained thieves that had perfectly executed a snatch and grab of over four million dollars worth of precious stones the month before, and he wanted to be sure that it wouldn't happen again. The thieves had been brazen and professional, and while it seemed unlikely that they would strike again so soon, it was better to be safe than sorry.

Hiring KSI had been the most logical decision.

They had all taken turns escorting Mr. Alexander York through his drops. Today it was Luca and Van's turn. Luca decided that he'd rather hang out on the rooftop than follow Mr. York around, standing in doorways looking intimidating wasn't his deal.

It was probably for the best. Luca was scarier than any of the criminals that jumped their client could have been. The client had wanted him dressed in a suit and dark glasses. Normally he followed instructions, but he wasn't in the mood today. He was feeling restless and since King had failed to remind him of the dress code, he had dressed down but kept the sunglasses. Mr. York hadn't said anything, but Van knew the client wasn't going to complain to a Kindred. He might hear about it from King later, but right now he didn't give a shit.

Van flanked their client. Standing in front of a secured door that Mr. York had just entered. He stood tall, his arms crossed over his broad chest, blocking the door effectively with his bulk.

Van knew that he looked scary as fuck. He was

hoping it would keep anyone with prying eyes moving along quickly. He scanned the crowd walking past him on the street. Under normal circumstances, the alcove he was in would be something he would avoid. He didn't want to get boxed in. But with Luca in the sky covering anyone entering his space, he was content to stand and wait.

These morning runs were easy. Luca was the one that thought setting up hours early was essential. He was already waiting at their client's first drop when Van arrived.

Van didn't know why he was restless. His job made him proud, and he did good work. It wasn't in him to sit still and not be in the middle of some kind of action, even when there wasn't any. When the jobs were clean and smooth, he still loved the adrenaline rush that his vigilance brought him. Using his bear's senses to their full advantage. The tenseness of his muscles, his hearing and eyesight searching for anything that could be perceived as a threat.

There wasn't anything he would change about his life. Except maybe having someone to share it all with. But that wasn't something he was willing to hold his breath waiting for. Besides, he had a life to live until fate decided to step in.

Van's hearing picked up the click of his client's footsteps moving towards the door. He stepped back, his fingers curling around the door handle. He gave one last glance to make sure that the area behind him was secure before bringing his body around to cover the opening door.

Mr. York was a middle-aged man that wore a three piece suit that fit him like a glove. His, appearance spoke of importance. Mr. York's eyes darted up in relief to Van's.

"Everything okay?"

"Of course, Mr. York."

"Good, good, I'm done for the day. I'd like to go back to my offices."

Van nodded. He could tell the case that his client had walked in with was heavier than when he had entered. York looked tense, and Van knew that his mind was on the contents of the case, and his memories of the heist. It hadn't been pretty, and the man had been lucky to escape with his life.

The pair headed towards the black SUV waiting at the curb. They had almost cleared the overhang of the building when Van's earpiece chirped.

"Incoming, nine o'clock. Could just be a transient, but he's moving fast."

Van kept moving, placing his body between the client and the possible threat. His eyes slid over to see a slight man wearing a black sweatshirt with the hood pulled up. The man's face was obscured by the hood and chunks of lank hair that were falling forward as he moved.

"What's..." Mr. York started to ask.

"Get in the vehicle, Mr. York, shut the door when you're inside," Van ordered.

The hooded man sped up and Van could smell his desperation as he got closer. Rank and sour.

Yanking the SUV door open, Van gave Mr. York a shove, and the man yelped as he went headfirst across the back seat. Van wasn't able to shut the door before the hooded man was on him.

Van saw the small black handgun as it was pulled from the front pocket and his reflexes took over. He slapped the man's hand aside as Van grasped the gun with his other hand, spinning the man around and wrenching his arm behind his back.

The man swore in surprise as Van pulled hard enough to make the bones in his wrist creak.

"Are you alone?" Van asked as he shoved the gun into his front pocket.

"Nope," the man laughed without humor.

"Luca? Eyes?"

"Nothing yet. Possible second suspect coming from the opposite side. He bolted when he saw you. I think this was it."

"Can you call it in?"

"On it," Luca responded.

Van kept the man in just enough pain, his shoulder was probably on fire the way it was angled back, but it kept him compliant. Reaching for a pair of handcuffs, he secured the man.

Luca would be calling in to the Seattle Police Department. That meant Van's morning had just gotten longer. He would be at least another hour answering questions and filing reports. Luckily for him, he knew enough people in the department that the routine wasn't new to him.

"SPD is four minutes out. Soon as they arrive I'm gonna head out. You got this?" Luca asked.

"Yeah man, I'll secure the client and meet you back at the office."

"I'll be there."

Van didn't bother offering Luca a ride. The shifter was often vague about his whereabouts. Maybe he liked it that way. He was always a bit of a loner, but Van knew there were few men he'd want to have at his back. Odds were good that Luca was after the other man that he'd seen. Van had no doubt that he'd meet the smelly man's accomplice down at the station. Luca wasn't the type to abandon a lead like that.

The man Van held against the side of the SUV squirmed. Van kicked out the back of his knee making the man fall onto the sidewalk.

"Careful there, you don't want to get hurt."

"Fucker! You don't know who you're messing with."

"Clearly I'm messing with someone that thought he could rob a man in broad daylight, a man who clearly has a security detail. That tells me that I'm messing with a stupid motherfucker. And don't think we don't know about your friend. He might have abandoned you, but we'll get him, so don't worry about being lonely when you're behind bars."

CHAPTER 3

S eattle. The Emerald City it was once called. That was a long time ago, a time before the city had turned into the metropolis it now was. Van, a member of Clan Rekkr, drove through the streets, dodging pedestrians rushing across the street on their way to work. He'd woken up still itching for something. The previous day's failed robbery had only managed to distract him from his unsettled state for a few hours.

Van could only hope that today's assignment held something to keep him occupied. He needed something mentally and physically to help him burn off whatever was looming in the back of his mind.

The cool spring morning brought a light layer of fog that stretched over the streets. Van smiled as he passed the light-rail trains crisscrossing the city next to the freeway. Even with the city's massive public transit infrastructure, people still loved their cars.

When the Kindred Alliance decided to base its operations in Seattle the town was little more than a sawmill with shanty houses clinging to the hillsides. Now you could hop a high-speed train and be in Vancouver in forty minutes and the Seattle metro area stretched from Vancouver to Portland. It was hardly a sleepy mill town anymore.

But the Kindred Alliance and the United States Government had kept building their facilities, one after another. The politicians, not wanting the KA to gain too much power, unofficially moved most of their critical departments to the city by the Sound. Not that they really had that much control over the spread of the Kindred, they just wanted to make sure that they were involved in any decisions that might occur.

Those that could turn into animals, the ones that called themselves the Kindred, had been around as long as humans. The Kindred were always tougher, always faster, and their natural abilities provided them elite positions in all facets of the world.

The Kindred had never used their power to take over the human world, even though it would have been easy to stage a successful coup in any country.

Fortunately for the humans, the Kindred Councils wanted peace, and wanted to help build the world they were living in. So, a truce, at least in the power department, had been made. The Kindred were better at certain things, and it benefited the humans to encourage it. Concessions and compromises were made on both sides, and everything ran relatively smoothly.

The world was a mix of humans and Kindred. They worked together, lived together, and for the Kindred, at least most of them, it was with the humans that they found their mates. Mates that would be able to bear Kindred children. Those that found their mates inside the Kindred population had a purpose that meant more than creating biological offspring. The Kindred knew that who their mates were wasn't up to them. The Great Mother decided that for each person, and sometimes she had a wicked sense of humor. All they could do was be patient, and when the mating call came... that was when the real work began.

Van wasn't concerned about finding a mate. His time would come, he was confident of that. He didn't go for those dating websites that some Kindred used to try and find their human mates. He wasn't even that concerned that his mate might not be human. The Great Mother would tell him when and where it was going to happen for him. There was no need for him to push the issue. Although he wouldn't mind a few more years doing the job he loved. In his line of work, worrying about a mate and family would be distracting. And that was the last thing he needed.

Van pulled into a parking garage just off 5th Avenue in downtown Seattle. He turned right until he reached the floor two levels down that was solely reserved for King Security International. He pulled up next to a large black SUV, the kind King usually drove. He liked to lecture Van on the supposed benefits of driving a low profile, non-recognizable car. Van disagreed and continued to drive his Lexus LC500 through the streets of Seattle. The blistering yellow vehicle drawing every eye as it went by. People knew his car, they knew who he was. Whether they were impressed or scared, he didn't know or care. He didn't want anyone being sure exactly who he was or what he did.

Out of habit, he gave the parking area a quick sweep with his eyes to make sure he was the only one there before punching the elevator call button. The door opened and he pressed his security card against the reader and selected King Security's floor. The entirety of the tenth floor was secured, and if you made the mistake of trying to reach the floor without an appointment, you would get the sharp end of the King Security receptionist who played the triple role of office manager, nanny, and gatekeeper.

As the elevator rose, Van knew that his boss would be waiting for him with his office door open. He would have had eyes on him from the moment he turned down the street towards their building. He would have known when he had entered the garage, the elevator, and probably watched him walk into the office.

King was a nosy fucker and he loved his security cameras.

But then he was the best in the business. Everyone knew that King of Clan Rekkr could get the job done.

The doors opened and Van stepped out of the elevator into the King Security waiting room. An obnoxiously upbeat pop song was playing quietly over the sound system. The seating area was set with a dark brown couch and moss green side chairs crowded around a coffee table with the requisite array of magazines fanned out on its polished mahogany surface. The area was spotless and comfortable.

Directly across from the seating area was a large counter with the company insignia emblazoned across the front. Behind that massive desk sat a pale woman with white-blonde hair. She stared at him with the hint of smile in her eyes. The desk itself was at least six inches off the ground and Nadia sat on a high chair, almost looming over the reception area. Kindred could talk to her eye to eye, but humans had to look up, it was the way she liked it.

"Nadia," he said without slowing his walk. "Can't we change the music?"

"Van," she replied, quiet and crisp. "No, we can't. It's Bliss Hartley and I love her. Coffee's on the counter."

Van smiled, knowing that when he swung by the breakroom he would find a mug of coffee made exactly the way he liked waiting for him. It would be hot and perfectly flavored. He never asked Nadia how she knew; he just accepted that she did.

Nadia had been with the agency since its inception and was its most obvious secret weapon. She was young and small, almost frail looking, but it was hard to tell exactly how old she was because of her fairy-like appearance. Despite all of that, she was a force to be reckoned with.

Van turned left down the hallway seeking out the break room and found his coffee waiting for him on the counter just as it should be. He grabbed the mug and walked back past the reception area on his way to King's office. As he passed the entrance to the waiting area, he heard Nadia on a call.

"I don't give a shit, Cliff. I ordered those smoke bombs three weeks ago. What do you want my guys to do, light fires and wave their arms in the air? I ordered the goods, I've fucking paid for them, and I want them here now!"

Van didn't bother looking at her as he walked past. He knew that the moment anyone else came into the office quiet, timid Nadia would be greeting them. She was a mystery, that was for damn sure. He marveled at the way she was hiding two very different women in that tiny frame. One was a terrifying ball-buster, and the other was a sweet young woman who remembered everyone's coffee preferences without asking.

Just as he'd suspected, King's office door was open. He walked in without knocking and found his boss and best friend sitting in a high back leather chair, his back turned to him.

King was staring at a bank of screens lined up on the wall. There were a number of different views. Streets down below the building. One that looked like the inside of a vault. A few hallways that Van knew were a part of the surveillance gigs they had people on. And another that was the pool of an apartment building. I wasn't sure what the point of that one was. Extra-curricular interests maybe.

Dropping into a leather chair across from the desk, Van kicked his feet up and crossed them at the ankle. He took a noisy sip of his coffee as he waited for King to acknowledge them.

"Get your fucking feet off my desk, asshole."

Van didn't move.

"Why? You don't want your fancy desk to get messed up?"

"No, your feet smell."

Van knew that was a lie. They were both bear shifters. Like everyone that worked for King as a security specialist or bodyguard. Bodily hygiene was never an issue. King was just pushing his buttons.

It never worked, but that didn't mean King ever tired of testing him. Van had hardened himself over the years and he didn't let anything rattle him. His time in the military had taught him discipline and growing up in his clan taught him why he needed to be successful.

"My feet don't smell. What's up your ass today? Why can't you make Nadia change the music in reception? Don't you think it's unprofessional to have that crap music pumping through the speakers?"

The chair spun around and King glared at him.

He was older than Van and his hair had the slightest gray at the temples. He was still a virile and formidable foe, and only the dumbest of their marks tried to cross him. Kindred were strong; they had skills that humans just didn't possess. It's what made them so good at their jobs. Better than good, it made them the only ones people called when they needed their kind of specialized services.

"No, I can't. She takes care of this office top to bottom and is good at her job. She doesn't talk about our business to anyone she shouldn't and she anticipates my needs. If I didn't need meatheads like you, all I'd need is her and AJ to keep the computers running."

Sorting through the papers on his desk, King picked up a folder. "I need you to pick up a job. Anson is on vacation, but he's due back anytime. Luca is supposed to check in this morning and Zion is still out on that undercover job. I might be able to get Hudson to assist, but I'm not sure."

Van shrugged, he didn't mind going solo. "What's the gig?"

King threw a folder across the desk to him. "Chaz Dillard. And yes, that's his real name. His business practices are suspect at best. I've heard his name thrown around before. He's a dick, but that's not the point."

"What *is* the point?"

"His fiancée was kidnapped."

Van raised his eyebrow, surely a kidnapping would require a bit more urgency than what King was displaying right now.

"He just figured it out," King said, tenting his fingers together.

"How long has she been gone?" Van flipped open the folder. A picture of the woman was paper clipped to the file folder. She was beautiful, with red hair and clear skin. Her blue eyes held humor and sweetness. How could anyone not notice that this woman was missing, and more importantly, how would they not be tearing the city apart trying to find her?

"Five days."

Van's eyes snapped up to meet King's. "Five days and he's just *now* coming to us?" He couldn't imagine that. If the woman you were intending to marry had been kidnapped, or put in harm's way. God only knows how she was being treated, and they were just hearing about it now?

"He thought she'd split on him. He was giving her time to 'come to her senses,' that's what he told me. He didn't think there was anything to worry about until he got a voicemail demanding a ransom."

Van snorted, "Seriously? Voicemail? Who does that?"

"Dumbasses. Here's the recording," King said, hitting a button on his keyboard. One of the video screens behind him turned black and the recording played over the speaker next to his computer.

Someone was trying to disguise their voice and doing a terrible job of it. The guy on the other end of the phone actually cleared his throat a few times and Van couldn't help but chuckle.

"Yeah, we've got your fiancée." The man mispronounced fiancée. "We want one million dollars in a black bag left under the bench in Gas Works Park. You have twenty-four hours." Another voice mumbled in the background and then the call clicked off.

"So… they want money left out in public, under any number of benches, they didn't prove they had her, and they called in on a traceable line?"

"Yeah, that's why I figured you could handle this yourself. I bet you could get her without these morons even noticing. Simple extraction."

Van scanned the notes in the folder. The call had been traced back to an industrial complex. He knew the area well and knew that the buildings in it were barely secured. It would be a quick job. He didn't care about punishing the idiots that had kidnapped her, that wasn't what he was hired for. In this case, he was just a delivery boy. Secure package, deliver package.

Standing up, Van slapped his hand on the folder. "I'll suit up and see if I can get this done before lunch."

"Cocky bastard. If I didn't know you could handle this alone, I'd make you wait for backup."

"I'll have her back before dinner."

"I'm sure her loving fiancé will be happy to hear that."

Van didn't comment because he couldn't imagine losing someone that important for five days and not thinking to alert someone. If what King had said about this Chaz character was right, it also didn't surprise him that this individual hadn't gone to the police. That usually meant that they didn't want the authorities looking over their shoulder into their personal business. That's where King's agency came in. King's code of ethics were his own and Van had never questioned his boss' decisions. The world didn't always work on the straight and narrow. It was often messy and underhanded, and that's where they stepped in.

When someone needed protection, they called in a bear. Financial advice? Find yourself a wolf. If you needed something found out, that was where the big cats came in. That's just how the world worked, and it suited them just fine. There was plenty of crossover in jobs, not every bear was cut out for protection, and not every wolf was great with numbers. Nothing was set in stone, but often the species played out their individual strengths.

"You know, I need a vacation," Van said standing up and cracking his knuckles.

"You need to get laid."

Van snorted. He didn't need to get laid. He had hit the age in a shifter's life that his animal didn't want anyone to touch him anymore. As a youth, he'd sought it out eagerly. Anything to feed the beast. Now he was more likely to step aside when a woman got too close to him. It literally rubbed him the wrong way. His animal didn't want some random woman's scent on him. He didn't want anyone else thinking he was claimed. It shouldn't matter what anyone thought, but it did to him.

He laughed harshly. "You're one to talk. I'll head out unless you have anything more for me?"

"Nothing urgent. Stay safe and try to not blow anything up."

"Hey, Prague wasn't entirely my fault. That leopard gave me bad intel. And I didn't know that those tanks were full of propane."

"Uh-huh. Check in when you're on your way. I'll have Nadia on standby for your call."

Van nodded and headed out to grab his gear. King Security's gear vault was a large room full of every possible piece of equipment or tactical gear a protection specialist could need, plus a full armory containing guns, ammo, and explosives. The guns weren't entirely necessary in their line of work. Most of the time they were hired for bodyguard duty, which involved a lot of standing around waiting for something to happen that never did. But it didn't hurt to be prepared.

After checking his standard sidearm and extra clips, he strapped a knife engraved with the rune of his clan against his shin, and tucked another backup one at the small of his back. He grabbed gloves that would protect from leaving fingerprints behind and also allow him to avoid contact with any bodily fluids. Once he had what he needed he headed out, giving a brief nod in Nadia's direction as he walked by.

"Don't forget your receipts," she called to him without looking up.

Van grunted and mumbled to himself, "Fucking receipts." That lady could throw him off with just a sentence. He was going on an op. Granted it was a cakewalk of an op, but it was still work and she was talking about receipts like he was going to stop for a mission critical mocha.

Being on the clock meant leaving his slick yellow beast in the company garage. A nondescript black SUV waited for him. Keeping a low profile was essential to the success of their business. Vehicles that blended in, license plates that were a series of numbers and letters that were virtually impossible to decipher at a quick glance. No vanity plates here.

Picking the first vehicle he came to in the garage, he typed in his code on the console and the engine started. He cruised through the streets of Seattle dodging in and out of traffic.

The easy flow of the traffic helped put his mind into work mode as he plotted out possible scenarios. Calculating the distance to the local hospital if his mark wasn't in a healthy state. What his plan would be if there was a warehouse full of thugs guarding her. These assholes could be just as dumb as they sounded, or it could be an elaborate set up to lure someone like him into a trap.

Van wasn't about to be that patsy.

CHAPTER 4

"Y ou fuckers hit me one more time and I swear to god I'll bite your dicks off!"

Cora didn't care that to be able to actually make good on that claim they would have to pull their pants down, it was the threat that counted. Besides, if they thought she was trouble now, they had no idea what they were in for if they tried anything close to sexual. She'd go Tasmanian Devil on their asses and tear them to pieces. She might be tied up and defenseless now, but she figured that with enough flailing and bared teeth, she could still do some damage.

"Why ain't your man paying up? We was told he'd pay." This came from Frack who had apparently grown tired of his babysitting duties and thought he should be somewhere counting his cash.

It was interesting that he said they were told Chaz would pay. It made sense that someone would have tipped them off to who she was, and how much Chaz could afford... they were too stupid to be acting alone and without orders.

When she'd called out for water, Frack had come into the room in an angrier mood than usual. He smelled like he'd been drinking and the stench of him made her want to gag. He came towards her and without a word slapped her hard across the face. She'd felt her lip smash against her teeth and tasted blood. The pain made her ears ring and eyes water. The large metal ring he had on his hand made direct contact with her mouth. The pain radiated over her jaw and she felt a wet trickle of blood drip down her chin. She saw the moment of shock on his face right before the evil gleam came into his eye. He liked it. Hitting her made him feel good. He drew back his hand again, but this time he didn't hit her with an open palm, he backhanded her. His knuckles struck her cheekbone hard. She would have a bruise to show for it. The flash of pain was followed by a strange numbness, but it was only a temporary blessing. Cora knew it was going to hurt later.

"Maybe you got the number wrong! Did you

ever check that he got the message?" she screamed back at him. She really didn't care that she shouldn't be yelling at him. Fuck him. Fuck Chaz.

Frack looked over at his partner in crime, who was leaning against the doorframe, but Frick just shrugged.

"Please tell me you actually talked to someone?" she asked. It hadn't occurred to her until that moment that her kidnapper's skill set might be even more pathetic than she had originally feared.

"We left a message, bitch. That's how people communicate. We didn't even ask for that much. What's a million bucks to that asshole?"

Cora started laughing even though the movement made her jaw ache, and caused her lip to brush roughly against her upper lip. The hilarity of the whole situation was overriding the pain.

"You think he has a million dollars just sitting around? Chaz's family is rich but not the way you're thinking. Their money is all tied up in businesses and property. Did you give him a way to contact you or even tell you if he had the money?"

There was silence from the idiots. Cora had a sinking feeling that she wasn't going to get rescued. The chance that Chaz hadn't checked his messages was a serious possibility. She had run away after all, so there was also a chance that Chaz was just pissed at her for taking off without saying anything. What if he wasn't looking for her at all? The bridal shop would have ratted her out immediately when she'd run off in their dress. She was screwed.

"Seriously, did either of you check if there was a drop? What if the money was there and it's been taken by someone else because you're too stupid to do anything right? Haven't you ever seen a kidnapping in a movie or on TV? For fuck's sake!"

The two looked at each other again. "You go check," Frick ordered. There didn't seem to be a clear leader between the two, and Frack appeared to take exception to being ordered around.

"*You* go check!"

Frack turned and stalked over to his partner. He gave him a shove. "I'm staying here. You go check."

Cora didn't want Frack to stay. His abuse was only going to escalate and she didn't want to end up more bruised and abused than she already was.

"Why don't you two take it outside and have a nice little chat about it? Better yet, give me a phone and I'll call Chaz and see if he even got your message!"

This was getting ridiculous. Now she was managing her own kidnapping.

"Bitch, don't tell me what to do!" Frack

screamed, spittle flicking from his lips. He was truly a disgusting human being.

Cora shrugged, trying to pretend that she wasn't terrified. The idiots talked quietly together, and then they glared at her and went back through the doorway, leaving her alone in the room. She spat a mouthful of blood onto the concrete floor.

"Well, looks like it's just me, myself and I again," she muttered, attempting to relax her shoulders. Her joints ached from being tied in this unnatural position. It was going to take a lot of chiropractic visits to fix the damage being done by these morons.

Leaning back, she closed her eyes as she rested her head against the pipe she was tied to. Cora kept thinking about what she should have done. First, she should have told Chaz she needed a break, just a week away from everything to get her bearings. Then he would have at least known where she was. Second, she should have checked into a nicer hotel that would have put their customer's security a little higher on the list than the Emerald Getaway Motel seemed to. It seemed that the choices she'd made over the last few days had led to a cluster fuck of epic proportions. All she had wanted was a break, some fried chicken and a bottle of champagne in a cheap hotel room. All by herself. When she'd gotten bored, she would have gone back and dealt with her shit. But now everything was so much more complicated.

More importantly though, there seemed to be a bigger game at play. Nothing about her kidnappers made her believe that they would even know who Chaz was let alone figure out how to find her. Honestly, nothing would have surprised her. She knew that there were plenty of people across the country that didn't like Chaz, or his family.

It didn't help that Chaz's family were a little cavalier in their business dealings, which meant that they sometimes did business with a small, but influential, group of companies that had been subversively trying to bring down the Kindred. She couldn't understand why these company owners had a problem with Kindred. It would never work without both parties. If Kindred failed, humans failed.

In the beginning, it appeared that there had been much more of a division between the species. Anything different was always seen as bad or scary. But the Kindred needed humans, and soon humans realized that working together made life much more livable. Not every family had a Kindred relative, but there were plenty now that did. In private Chaz would sneer at the Kindred. But he liked money more than he liked sticking his nose up at the shifters. He didn't want Cora to associate with them, but that was almost impossible. Kindred were a part of every aspect of daily life.

Cora let out a sigh and ran her tongue over her damaged lip. "Well, at least if they kill me, I won't have to get married."

⚜

Van pulled his SUV up to the dilapidated warehouse and cut the engine. He pulled out his Glock checking that there was a round chambered. He always dressed in black cargo pants and a plain black t-shirt when he went out on a job, and there were extra clips stashed in the pockets of his light Kevlar vest. It wasn't a full bulletproof number, but it would provide protection against knives or shivs, he could shift if anything got crazy. This was how he liked to operate. Quick and clean. He hated suit gigs; there was nothing more impractical than being trapped in a suit when it came to dodging bullets or running after a perp.

His quick drive around the building showed him there was only one vehicle so no one would be sneaking up on him. There were no lookouts, no cameras, not even a hint of protection around the place. He stepped out of the vehicle and sniffed the air.

No scent of gun oil, or explosives, just the left over smells of some kind of fish or seafood processing plant. There was no excessive noise coming from the building, nothing was on or running. In fact, there was hardly any noise at all. His Kindred senses made his job that much easier, but it didn't take a good nose to realize that the building was all but abandoned.

He did a quiet sweep of the surrounding area and found a back door that was already ajar. These guys were rank amateurs. Emphasis on the rank. Sometimes Kindred senses weren't a blessing.

He listened for a moment before opening the door, and then he slipped inside and wound his way through a corridor lit by a stereotypical flickering fluorescent light. Leaks in the roof and pipes had left small pools of water on the floor that he stepped over carefully.

He stopped at a door that had a glass window on the upper half. Voices were coming from inside. Two men arguing over who was going somewhere. Where they were going, they didn't say, and Van didn't care. He took a deep breath and only smelled two unwashed bodies.

Van didn't give a shit about these two morons, he had a single objective. Find his target, extract her safely and and return her to her loving fiancé. The easiest paycheck he'd collect all year.

Crouching low and moving past the door, he continued down the hallway to another door that looked like it had been reinforced at one point. But that had been a long time ago, now it was just a heavy obstacle. Trying the handle, he found that it wasn't even locked. There was the faintest sound of breathing coming from the other side. He pulled the door open as quietly as possible and scanned the room before entering, staying low to the ground and moving quickly.

The room was mostly empty. A few crates scattered around with a rusted metal desk in the corner. He zeroed in on the sound of breathing and walked cautiously towards the sound. Around a corner, he found a young woman asleep, leaning against a thick metal pipe. Her dark red hair fell over her face, and even in the dim light, her ivory skin glowed. She was pretty. Scratch that, she was stunning. But that wasn't important right now. Right now he saw that her arms were tied behind her back and she was slumped over in what must have been an uncomfortable position. The wedding dress she wore was torn and filthy and her dirty bare feet peeked out from under the hemline.

He took a moment to assess her condition. His

eyes went straight to the blood at her lip and the purple bruise and swelling around her right eye and cheek. They'd hit her.

Van felt rage rising up inside him. He could tolerate a lot in the world. People were shit and he never was surprised by it. But hitting a woman was intolerable. These asshats hit a woman that couldn't even defend herself.

"Ms. Butler?" he said, his voice low but not a whisper. He didn't give a shit if those guys heard him now, he just didn't want to startle her.

"Ms. Butler, I'm Van. I'm here to get you out of this shithole." He didn't want to say 'rescue' because he wasn't Prince-fucking-Valiant. He also knew that there were enough humans out there looking hard for a Kindred rescuer. Kindred groupies were a fact of life and Van had become very cautious to not even utter that phrase as it seemed to spark a reaction in a lot of females. He'd learned that the hard way.

The woman sniffed, her nose crinkling. She tried to straighten up, and then grimaced in obvious pain. That made him want to hurt someone. Her eyes blinked a few times and then a pair of blue eyes focused in on him.

"You have a van?" she asked groggily, her eyes showing her confusion. On top of having just been woken up, she was in pain and probably dehydrated.

"No, my name is Van. I'm here to get you. I'm going to untie you and then I want you to wait here for me."

"Did Chaz send you?"

Van reached around her cautiously not wanting to startle her. She accepted that he wasn't there to hurt her and that made him feel good, while at the same time he wanted to lecture her on not trusting strange men.

"He hired my company, yes." Van untied her hands and helped her up. She groaned as he helped her stand.

"You okay?" Stupid question but it had to be asked.

"Peachy. I'm cold, dirty, and hungry. My shoulders feel like shit, my face hurts and I'm really pissed about this dress getting ruined. I actually liked it," she said, pulling at a piece of torn lace.

"Your dress?"

Her blue eyes flashed up at him in anger. "This was a nice dress! I liked this dress. It made me happy. It made me feel good! Even though no one else would have appreciated it on me." Her voice rose angrily as she spoke. "It was pretty and now it's ruined because of those assholes!"

Great. Van didn't really want a hysterical woman on his hands, no matter how pretty she was. "Okay then. But you might want to keep your voice down. Those meat bags are still in the other room and I was going to leave them, but seeing your face has changed my mind. Still, I'd like to get the upper hand on them. Don't much feel like getting shot today."

"My face? What's wrong with my face?" she demanded.

"Looks like you lost a fight, that's what. I think those two need a reminder not to hit women."

She squinted at him. "Why don't you also remind them not to kidnap them, tie them up and leave them to starve?"

"I'll add that to the list. You gonna wait here?"

"Where the hell am I going to go?" She tried to throw her hands up in the air but gasped as the pain shot through her shoulders and she dropped them with a glare.

Van grunted and turned on his heel. He didn't look back to make sure Ms. Butler was still there. He had the keys to the SUV so she'd be walking if she didn't want his help.

CHAPTER 5

H e was *Kindred.*

　　She had been dreaming about spicy pan-fried noodles. She was hungry and most of her dreams the last few days had been about food. On the plus side, she was probably a few pounds lighter and if the dress hadn't been trashed, she'd would have been thrilled about having to have it taken in.

Instead, she was rudely pulled away from the sesame lullabies that were bringing her a little happiness by someone shaking her and calling her name.

Cora was proud of herself that she didn't gasp when she saw the man crouching down in front of her. His eyes were gray and cold, but it wasn't the gray color that made her aware of what he was. It was the incandescent shine of his eyes reflecting back at her that did it. The kind of eyes you see staring out at you from the dark when an animal was stalking you.

She'd been fascinated by those eyes since she was a little girl. It was the mark of a shifter. They couldn't hide their eyes. This man, Van, was big too. She would have guessed he was a shifter even without seeing his eyes. When he stood in front of her after releasing her hands, he towered over her, well over six feet tall. The black shirt he was wearing was also stretched tight over his thickly muscled arms and chest, and the vest he was wearing didn't hide much.

If she had to guess, she would think he was a bear. They tended to be some of the biggest of the Kindred, and for good reason. Their jobs were as dangerous as their animals.

Even though they worked and lived with humans side by side, there were always secrets about them. They liked it that way. They didn't share with those outside their clans. Unless you were mated to one, of course. She'd known plenty of women whose lifelong dream was to be mated to a shifter. It was almost cult-like.

Cora never thought that she would be one of those women. Everyone knew Kindred only mated with humans to continue their species. Two dominant shifters couldn't make a child. It just never worked. It didn't mean there weren't shifter couples; they just tended to be childless or adopted to expand their family.

But once you were a Kindred mate, you were in on all the secrets, whatever those might be.

Leaning against the wall waiting for Van to return, Cora scratched at her hair. She needed a shower ASAP. Just the thought of the layer of dirt on her skin made her want to scratch at her head again.

She hadn't been waiting to be rescued. Honestly, she'd thought that her best bet was that her captors would be happy with whatever money they got and let her go. Hopefully untying her first and not just leaving her to rot in the warehouse. The fact that Chaz had hired someone honestly surprised her a bit. Maybe he'd gotten some kind of discount. Were there coupons for this stuff?

When she'd run she hadn't really thought about what she was going to do next. Now she was going to have to figure something out. It didn't seem like Van was the type to just leave her at another hotel, he'd deliver her back to Chaz. That meant she was going to have to go back and face whatever the hell was supposed to happen next. Great.

She could call her parents, but moving back to Texas didn't appeal to her. She loved Washington and had picked it for college purely because it wasn't so hot in the summers. It wasn't the degree programs or the school ranking. She was just tired of being hot all the time.

A crashing noise echoed down the hall, making her jump. There was another sound like glass breaking and she was pretty sure she heard a howl of pain. Cora froze, flattening herself against the wall. She briefly thought about running in to help, but that was ridiculous. What help could a moderately sized woman in a ruined wedding dress be to a Kindred? Some well-aimed slapping and maybe a swift kick in the shin?

Although, when Frack had hit her earlier, she was pretty sure she could have at least scratched his eyes out had her hands been free.

There was another dull thud from down the hall, and then a few moments passed before the man named Van came back through the door. He was brushing the back of his glove against his pants. She could see the wet smear of blood on them from where she was.

"Are they alive?" she asked as he got closer.

"Barely," he grunted.

"Are the cops on their way?"

"The client requested blackout. No cops."

Cora shook her head. *Of course.* Chaz wouldn't

want anyone thinking he was weak and having his fiancée kidnapped under his nose wouldn't make him look strong to his competitors. His father wouldn't have tolerated that either. It was probably Charles senior that made the call. Cleaning up after Chaz was a normal state of affairs. Money erased a lot of things.

"Shocker," she said humorlessly.

"Let's get you back to our offices. Unless you need medical attention?"

Cora shook her head. "Nope, just a shower and some food. Then maybe a long nap. Things I'm sure you aren't paid for."

"I'm paid to take you back to our offices so the client can be notified of your safe return."

"Well, don't try leaving him a message. He'll never get it. You can just drop me at my apartment. I live up on Second Street."

Van didn't respond. He scooped her up in his arms.

"What the hell? Put me down!"

"Your feet are bare," he said with a grunt.

"Exactly, they are already filthy and cold. What's a little more filthy and cold going to hurt?"

"You're not walking," he said fast stepping quickly out of the room.

"Do you have someplace to be?" she asked, bouncing in his arms.

He grunted again and kept walking as he answered. "I got shit to do. This shit is done and I want to do something else."

She made a choking noise. "You want to do something else? Well excuse me; I didn't realize my kidnapping interrupted your plans. Maybe you should have let someone else take the job. Not that Frick and Frack were expert thugs. Or maybe they picked you because they knew they couldn't do any real harm."

She was trying to goad him, and it was only working a little. "Looks like they were competent enough to harm you," he drawled.

"My hands were tied. It was a punk move to hit me. I could tell that the little shit liked it too. Wait, where is he? I wanna kick him in the balls," she demanded, turning in his arms.

"No ball kicking. They're hurting enough, believe me. Let's get you out of that dress, it stinks."

"You're saying I smell? Nice bedside manner. I could be emotionally scarred, terrified for my life, and you're telling me that I need a bath?!" Rude.

His eyebrow rose as she glanced at him. She took in those eyes again, they were shining at her. His hair was dark and cut short and the scruff on his jawline accentuated the lines of his face. She resisted the urge to brush her fingertips against his cheek.

"You scared?"

"What? No, I'm mad!"

"Good, mad is useful."

"Listen, Van whatever your last name is, I appreciate the manly intervention, but I'll be fine. I can take care of myself."

"Not gonna happen. Back to my office, contact the client, then you can do whatever you want. That's protocol, and I don't break the rules."

Oh, he really shouldn't have said that. It wasn't true. She'd given up a lot of her future to Chaz when she didn't break up with him after college. It was hard to admit, but being with him was better than dating. Being single was hard work. Chaz was... comfortable. Not passionate or exciting, but comfortable. They had a routine. It was no great love affair. Outside of their first year together, things had been... orderly. The fact that they hadn't had sex in a year should have been a much bigger clue she shouldn't be getting married.

"Fine, why don't you call his highness and tell him to meet me at my place?"

"You don't live together?"

Not that she needed to explain herself, she still answered. "I like my space."

Let him take what he wanted from that. She was a grown woman that didn't need to explain herself to any man. She was also a grown woman being carried in a wedding dress by the handsome Kindred that had just rescued her from a damn warehouse. All they needed was a triumphant theme song to play over a loudspeaker. He had rescued her though. He didn't do it because he wanted to or that he cared about her. He was just being paid. That was a legitimate reason.

Reaching the black monster SUV parked out front, he set her down gently before opening the back door. She climbed inside, pulling and tugging the poofy dress around her. It really wasn't practical. She finished and waited for him to close the door. As soon as he did, she moaned. She hurt. All over. A hot shower sounded like heaven.

Van got in, started the engine then leaned over to the glove box. He popped it open and grabbed something, and tossed it into her lap. He pulled open the center console and retrieved a bottle of water.

"Here."

She looked down at her lap and saw a bottle of ibuprofen. She wanted to reject it out of spite, but at the moment, the promise of a little relief was better than chocolate cake. Scrabbling at the top of the bottle, she shook out two pills and swallowed them down with the water, chugging it all down in record time.

"More?" he asked.

"No, I probably shouldn't have done that. Now my stomach hurts."

"Warn me if you're gonna yack. I don't want to have to detail this rig."

CHAPTER 6

Van gripped the steering wheel as he navigated through traffic. He'd been protecting himself when he said she smelled. Sure, the scent coming off her was of someone that had been left too long in a dank room, but it didn't cover her natural sweet scent. There were notes of her perfume still clinging desperately to her skin. He could smell her fear, her anger, everything that had happened over the past week. It confused him that he had even bothered to dig that deep. He kept pulling in deep breaths of her, tasting the different notes and separating them into the real her, and what was her experience.

He had a sudden urge to drive her to his loft and help her clean up. It was weird. He didn't let anyone come to his loft. He liked his solitude. Even when he had dated, he never took his dates home. It was his den and he didn't like anyone else intruding. He tried to shake off the thought of her walking through his house in that ridiculous dress, but it lingered just a little too long.

But Van had to admit that he liked her spirit. He'd almost given in when she had demanded to go kick those guys in the balls. He'd left them crumpled on the floor, both unconscious after he'd rearranged their teeth and made sure they had their fair share of broken ribs when they woke up. They wouldn't forget the beating and he hoped for their sake that in the future they'd think twice about taking jobs that involved hurting women.

"My office is downtown," he said, trying to start a conversation. It sounded awkward even to his own ears; but the silence that had settled over the car was more awkward.

"Okay."

She sounded exhausted. He glanced into the rearview mirror, adjusting it so that he could see her properly. Her eyes were closed, her head leaning back against the headrest. She was a beauty. Even under the dirt and stress of what she'd been through. To him, she looked like she was glowing. If he said that to her she'd probably remind him it was sweat.

It didn't matter, he could look past all that. Not

that he should be looking at her like anything other than a parcel that needed to be delivered.

Van couldn't think of anything else to ask her so he switched on the radio. As they got closer to the office, he dialed the front desk.

"King Security International, this is Nadia speaking."

"Nads, I need you to prep the recovery room. Order in some food and make sure there are clothes... size," he paused and looked into the mirror again scanning her briefly. "Medium?"

The sleeping figure in the back seat snorted. "Large, please," she said to the interior of the car.

"Got it, and Van, don't call me Nads."

The line clicked dead.

"Seriously, what the hell was that? Flattery?" she asked.

"What the fuck do I know about women's clothes?" he answered honestly.

She huffed and looked out the window. Then she started in on the questions. "What's your last name?"

"You know good and well I don't have one. What are you playing at?"

"Isn't it rude to ask a Kindred what their clan is?"

"No, is it rude for someone to ask you your family name?"

She shook her head. Her curious gaze on him and he held back the urge to squirm.

Damn, her eyes were distracting. "I'm Clan Rekkr. We're based out of Wyoming."

"I heard of Rekkr. It means warrior, right? Your clan is into oil or something, right?"

"We've been involved in the oil business, yes. Among other things."

"Are you mated?"

"No."

"Do you have a girlfriend?"

"Do you always ask this many personal questions?"

She paused for a moment. "No, but I don't get to be around Kindred much. Chaz doesn't think it's proper."

"What the fuck is that supposed to mean?" Van knew there were plenty that didn't like his kind. He didn't give them much thought. The majority of people accepted them and they lived happily together. But just as there were humans that didn't like the color of someone's skin, there were those that didn't like Kindred.

She shrugged. "He says his business associates like to work with humans. I think he's just intimidated by anyone bigger and stronger than him. He hates that you guys have cornered the market on so many things."

"Are you trying to make me hate this guy?"

He didn't need to ask that. He already did. Anyone who couldn't be bothered to look for the woman he was supposed to marry for days and then he hired someone else to take care of the problem for him wasn't worth his time anyway. Chaz wasn't at the King office pacing, worried out of his mind, punching walls because the woman he loved was gone. In fact, King hadn't even said that it was an in-person hire. He must have emailed or called.

That's not what a real man would do. A real man would fight and kill for his woman. At least that's what Van always assumed. Mated Kindred were fiercely protective of their mates and they didn't hesitate when it came time to defend them.

"He's not really a likable guy, so I don't have to try very hard."

"So why are you with him?" He couldn't believe he asked that. He didn't like sharing personal information with anyone. He figured the less people knew the better off he was. He didn't ask people about their lives unless it was useful intel to the mission.

She laughed quietly, maybe a little sadly, and looked out the window again. "Lazy? Comfortable? No, it's just that I've been with him so long that I forgot what it was like to be alone. The idea of being alone scared me. Then a few more years went by and I realized that even with him I was still alone, so what did I have to be afraid of?"

Van grunted in response. He knew loneliness. He had his clan and his friends at work. He hadn't lacked for female company when he was younger. He had thought more than once in the last few years that he was becoming too used to being by himself, but he'd never heard or felt the mating call. It wasn't there for him, and if he never got it, then that was what the Great Mother had planned for him. There would be a reason he was by himself.

"There are worse things than being alone."

"Sometimes it doesn't feel that way," she said quietly.

They rode in silence the rest of the way to the office. He opened her door in the parking garage and helped her out.

The ride up the elevator was silent. When the door opened, Nadia was waiting for them.

"I've got the room ready. I'll escort her if you don't need her anymore?" she said in her delicate voice.

"No, I've got calls to make."

"Wait," Cora said, putting her hand on his arm.

He resisted the urge to pull away. He didn't like

people touching him. His animal side rejected the idea of anyone having that much familiarity with him. But this time, the light touch of her hand on his arm didn't make him want to pull away. It was... okay for her to touch him.

"Can you give me a few minutes before you call him? I mean, I need to get cleaned up, I'd like to eat something. Chaz is probably too busy to come down here right away."

"Too busy to find out his fiancée has been rescued?"

She shrugged a little sadly, a motion that made him mad, and at the same time a little empty.

"Let's get you cleaned up," Nadia said quietly, gesturing towards the hallway.

Van let the receptionist lead her away to the recovery room. He watched them go, Cora in her bedraggled dirty wedding dress. It made a picture of desperation and angst that he would never forget.

CHAPTER 7

Van stomped into King's office and slammed the door behind him. King was in his chair, and a tall slender man with tanned skin, dark hair and dark eyes was leaning against the office wall. Luca.

Van knew the Kindred in King's office didn't like to have his back unprotected, and it wasn't unusual to see him take up this kind of position, especially in unfamiliar locations. It wasn't that he didn't trust King, he was just a cautious kind of guy. The tall man was hard faced and he kept a clean-shaven jaw. His clan was closer to the border with Mexico, their territory crossing over both sides on the human border. To date, Van had never seen the man smile.

Luca was the kind of man that no one, Kindred

or human, would mess with. He radiated a deadly kind of calm and Van remembered that Luca's skills were almost as legendary as King's. His lethal accuracy with a sniper rifle was never doubted, and his bear was silent and swift like a night wind. He was a force to be reckoned with.

"Luca," Van said as he sat.

"You know, we might have been discussing something important," King said drolly.

"Doubtful, Luca looks almost relaxed," Van said, kicking his feet up.

"Relaxed?" The word slithered out of Luca's mouth.

"You don't exactly look like you're in the middle of a hunt. You taking some time off?"

"Does it look like I go on vacation?" Luca asked with a smirk. That was the closest thing to a smile you'd get out of him.

"Maybe you should. I know you give *me* the creeps, I can't imagine your targets feel much differently. If Luca of Clan Othala was hunting me, I'd be shitting my pants. You owe us all a vacation."

King interrupted their banter. "Since your smart mouth is back in the office, I'm assuming that you've retrieved Ms. Butler?"

"Yeah, she's in the recovery room. Nadia is taking care of her."

"That reminds me," Luca said, stepping forward and pulling some papers from his back pocket. "Give these to Nadia."

King took them and shook his head. "You really need to learn to work with her."

"She doesn't like me. I don't mind. No need to ruin her day by talking to her. Besides, she makes that yelp noise when she sees me like I'm always startling her, that drives me nuts." Luca went back to his spot against the wall.

"Someone should call the client. Let him know that the contract is complete." Van broke into their important conversation about receipts.

King watched him, his eyes looking him over. "Someone?"

"Yeah, you've already communicated with him. I'm sure he'd want to hear from you."

"I'll make the call," King said, turning his chair from Luca to Van. "But it almost sounds like you don't want him to come and collect her."

"Cora asked for a few minutes to herself. Her captors were just as junior as we thought. But they did hit her." Van couldn't keep the growl out of his voice.

"You left them alive?" Luca asked, his voice was just as angry as Van was feeling.

"I did. Though not in the same shape I found them in. I was more interested in retrieving Cora."

"Cora is it?" King asked.

"It's her name," Van ground out.

King steepled his fingers, staring at him. "So, do I call him or not?"

"I think it can wait a little bit. He waited five days to report that she was missing... and he didn't even report it. He called us. He's not in a hurry, and she's not in a rush to get back to him." Van paused, letting his words sink in. "Has he even called to check on our progress?"

"No, he hasn't."

"Then he can wait," Van said standing up and storming out. He didn't like how King was staring at him. King was a master at studying people, and he didn't feel like being analyzed at the moment.

Marching past the room that he wanted to stop at, he kept going. He could smell the steam of the shower from the room. His mind cut to an image of Cora's wet body under the falling water. For some reason, he wanted to keep thinking of her. He wanted to imagine what her skin would smell like freshly washed and perfumed.

Perfumed? What the fuck was he thinking? He needed to remember that this was a job and it meant nothing to him delivering his mark to King. He didn't need to think about her anymore.

☙❧

Cora let the water from the shower soak into her hair. Her scalp itched from almost a week of not showering. The room Nadia the mouse had led her to was set up like a small studio apartment. She didn't think of Nadia as a mouse in a mean way. She was just such a delicate person. Quiet and pale, she looked like she couldn't hurt a fly.

The room was more like a miniature hotel suite. It had a single bed, and a couch that looked like it could actually be comfortable, not just a utilitarian piece of office furniture. The area included a small bathroom stocked with towels and soaps.

Nadia showed her the kitchenette and a mini-fridge full of water. She'd left a bag on the counter, a sandwich from a deli nearby.

Cora held herself back from tearing the bag open with her teeth. She didn't want to eat while she was still so dirty.

Once in the shower, her aches and pains came rearing up. Her face hurt and the joints of her shoulders felt like they were on fire.

She soaked for as long as she dared, never

running out of hot water. It was like heaven. She toweled off and wrapped herself in the fluffy towel. In the bathroom she pulled open drawers until she found packages containing brushes, toothpaste, a toothbrush and dental floss. It even had a hair tie and some bobby pins in it. Once she wrangled her hair up and out of the way, she kept opening cupboards until she found lotion and deodorant. She used the items then left them on the counter. They would probably be disposed of anyway after she left.

The disgusting remains of the ruined wedding dress had been removed while she showered, and a small stack of clean clothing sat on the end of the bed. Someone, probably Nadia, had left a pair of sweatpants and a t-shirt, both with a KSI logo on them. She slid them on and put on the hoodie that matched the pants. The bustier she'd worn under the wedding dress had also disappeared, but that was probably for the best. With no other alternative, she settled for braless and zipped up the hoodie. On the floor by the bed she found a pair of flip-flops that were a size too big but better than nothing.

Warm, clean, and safe, Cora let out a sigh of relief as she opened the deli bag and removed the sandwich. Taking it and a bottle of water back to the bed, she sat down on it cross-legged. Eating in bed was a cardinal sin in Chaz's house. She didn't know how long she had until Chaz showed up and she wanted to enjoy the last few moments of being on her own as long as possible.

The first bite of the sandwich was possibly the best thing she'd ever tasted. She took another big bite and sighed as she chewed. She was able to get enough food into her that she didn't feel the need to panic and shove it all in. Taking a breath she let the food settle as her stomach cramped.

There was a knock at the door. Chewing past the bite she mumbled, "Come in."

The door opened slowly and Van stuck his head in. Cora hadn't forgotten in the last few minutes how handsome he was. It didn't keep her from wanting to gasp at his appearance. His rough short beard made his jaw look even stronger. His reflective eyes shone, and she loved how they flashed at her.

"Am I interrupting?" he asked.

"No, just trying to not inhale this sandwich. I'm sure it would make me sick if I did. Come on in."

He walked in and closed the door behind him. He stepped towards the bed and held out a small blue gel pack.

"I thought you might need this for your cheek and eye. I also brought some antibiotic ointment for your lip. I don't think it will scar, but it wasn't clean."

"No, it wasn't. Have a seat. I'll use that when I'm done. Food is my priority right now."

He sat next to her and looked at her face. "That hurt?" he said gesturing towards her cut lip.

She had gone back to her sandwich. "A little." It did, but what was a little cut in the grand scheme of things.

She lifted her sandwich to her mouth again and saw him hesitate. He looked at her like he was unsure, then he lifted the ice pack he'd brought in and held it to her face. She jerked back as he touched her, and a look of worry crossed his handsome face.

"Sorry, did that hurt?"

"No, it's just cold."

He placed the pack back against her cheek and gruffly told her, "Eat."

She did as she was told because this big man was a little scary, but he was also being very sweet. She didn't know what to make of him.

"Why are you being nice to me? Is it like a package deal? Rescue and coddling all for one price?"

Van smirked at her. "You know, I don't think anyone has ever said I coddled them before."

"You're good at it," she said quietly.

"I don't like to see women hurt."

"I'm sure you've seen it before."

He was quiet and didn't say anything.

"When will Chaz be here?"

"I haven't called him yet. And neither has King."

She put the sandwich down and reached up to take the ice pack from him. Their hands brushed each other and she could have sworn she felt his hand twitch at the contact.

Keeping the ice pack pressed against her face, she looked down at her knees. "Is there any way you could... could you maybe not call him?"

"Why?"

"Because I don't want to go back," she admitted. "Did he tell you that I was missing before they kidnapped me?"

"I got the gist that you were gone for a few days."

"I ran away," she admitted. Cora didn't want to admit that. It made her sound weak. "I was in a motel room. I spent two days watching television and eating fried chicken." She looked away from him because he didn't seem like the type to her that would ever run from anything.

"Did he hurt you?" The question held barely disguised anger.

Cora shook her head. "No, Chaz doesn't pay enough attention to me to hurt me. He's just busy. I knew that about him. I'm not surprised or anything. His dad always intended for him to take over the family business. I knew that he was going to be distracted and away from home a lot. I held off my own career to support him. Now I don't know what I'm supposed to do with my life. I forgot that I had a choice too. When I was trying on the wedding dress, I realized that it was the first time I had been happy in a really long time and it scared the shit out of me."

"You know you have a choice, right?"

"You don't know Chaz."

"I know his type, Cora."

"Then you won't call him?"

He shook his head this time. "We finished the job. That means I have to call him, but it doesn't mean you have to go with him."

"He pays for my apartment. He pays for everything really. I wouldn't even know where to start if I broke up with him."

"You have family?"

"Out of state, yeah."

"Friends?"

Cora shrugged. "Nobody that isn't friends with Chaz and his family. I'm sorry I'm dumping all of this on you. I know it's not your problem. You can call Chaz, but would you mind giving me a head start? I want to get back to my apartment. Tell him I'm there, that would be okay."

She watched him struggle with something. "If you're sure," he finally said.

Cora gave him a sad smile. "We all have burdens to bear. This is mine. Maybe this experience will be the boost I need to get my ass in gear and change a few things. I do appreciate you rescuing me. I know it was a job, but it doesn't mean you weren't putting yourself in danger to do it."

"Today wasn't a big deal. Besides, I enjoyed beating up those guys. I'm guessing they had it coming."

"Model citizens they weren't," she agreed.

"Can I give you a ride back to your place? I want to make sure you get home safe."

"I can call a service, it's not a big deal."

"They kidnapped you once. There's a chance they'll try again."

Cora didn't want to go through that again. It had been scary, painful, and infuriating. She had so much to process right now.

"I really need to be alone." She said that because Van was too much for her to take in. His presence made her mind fuzzy. He was radiating so much sex that she could practically taste it. He probably didn't know that he had that effect on women, or maybe he did. But whether it was Van or the fact he was Kindred, she didn't care. It was too much for her. She was tired. Tired from her ordeal, tired from her thoughts ticking away trying to figure out her next step.

"Let me go back and check in with my boss. I'll arrange a ride for you. Someone that I trust to take you home. I'll also see if your fiancé has arranged for further protection for you. I'm sure he has and it will help set your mind at ease."

Cora didn't want to laugh at him. He was being so serious. It seemed like he was actually worried about her. It was nice.

"Thank you, really."

He nodded and left the room, closing the door behind him.

Cora looked down at her sandwich and her stomach churned. She'd have to talk to Chaz. He wouldn't be happy. He probably wouldn't listen to her the first time either, so she'd have to repeat herself over and over. The thought of what she still had to go through made her even more tired. Pushing the sandwich away, she curled up on her side on the bed and let the tears fall.

CHAPTER 8

"She needs a ride," Van rasped as he walked into King's office.

"Are you ever going to knock?"

King was looking out the window at the city skyline, a glass of brown liquid in his hand.

"Do I ever?"

"So our retrieval is doing okay?"

"No, she's not fucking okay. She wants to go home. She doesn't want to wait for her asshole fiancée to pick her up."

King turned around at that. "She doesn't want to wait here?"

"No, she doesn't want to be around him at all," Van said, planting his hands on his hips.

"That's hardly our business."

"Isn't it?"

"No, we got hired to do a job. We did the job, we're done. Don't make this into something it's not, Van. Don't make it personal."

Van started pacing. "Don't make it personal? That dickwad doesn't give a shit that she's even safe. He doesn't care. She's hurt and scared and where the fuck is he?"

"He's wherever he feels he needs to be. Not our problem. Make the call."

"She doesn't want to wait. Did he even arrange for surveillance? Coverage of any kind? She should have a bodyguard on her at all times. He can fucking afford it." Van was letting his anger get the better of him. He could feel his claws starting to elongate from his fingers. He could feel his neck thickening and his canines dropping in his mouth.

"Pull it back, I don't want the furniture damaged," King growled, his voice resonating through the room.

"I'm pissed!" Van growled.

"I get that, but I don't see why. She's nobody to you. Mr. Dillard made no further arrangements for her security. I will be happy to discuss those options with him when I report back to him about our successful retrieval. If he chooses not to continue to do business with us then that's the end of it."

"Fuck that! It's not the fucking end! She's still in danger!"

"Lots of people are in danger, Van. You want to burn off some energy, go ask Luca to shift and spar with you, but do it in the gym. I'm not remodeling again because you can't keep it together."

"She's different! She's got no one to look out for her."

Van tried to pull his animal back. He would need to find Luca later. If he didn't get his animal under control he would hurt the next person that looked at him funny.

"You going to make that your problem?"

Van didn't have an answer to that. He knew that he wasn't making any sense. He never cared about his clients. Never got emotionally attached to his marks. He didn't know why this one bothered him so much, why she made him feel weak. He'd never felt that in his life. He'd always been strong. His clan had raised him to be tough, capable, and above all to be successful. In his clan being successful meant having a job that benefited everyone that belonged to Clan Rekkr. They were one, and that meant they looked out for each other and lifted each other up.

Everything he did represented his clan. He

wanted his actions to lift not only his family, but King's business as well. Leaving Cora to the wolves, as it were, didn't seem like something that would bring him honor.

"No, I'm not saying it's my job. I'm saying it's our job. That's what we do."

King gave a laugh. "We handle shit, ours and other peoples. That's what we do. I like doing it and so do you. You need to take a step back and let this go."

Van knew he was right. It didn't feel right but the words were on point. Why this one redheaded woman was making him so crazy wasn't making any sense. He'd done a hundred jobs like this and he never thought about them once he was done. He just moved on to the next. Simple, clean, and efficient.

"Just have Luca take her home. Have him sweep the area and then wait around to make sure someone comes to see her."

"Really? You want to go tell Luca what to do?"

"Aren't you his boss?"

"Yes, just like I'm yours. I give orders, but only because I know you take it more as direction than a command. If you're so worried about her, you take her," King said.

Luca walked back into the room sweaty from working out. "Take who?"

"Client. Can you take her back to her apartment? Make sure she's safe?" Van asked.

Luca looked between the two men. "I'm not getting in the middle of you two. King?"

"If Van wants to babysit, let him do it," King replied.

"I don't want to babysit. She's in danger."

"Exactly. Her man hasn't arranged for further protection. If that changes I'll let you know. Until then, do what you want," King said, taking his seat.

Van wanted her watched, but he didn't want to be the one to do it.

"Fine, make the call," he said then stormed out.

As the door closed Luca turned from watching him leave.

"What the fuck was that?"

"That was a man not willing to listen to his animal and lashing out like a cranky cub."

"Who's this mark?"

"Not sure, but Ida told me that he was supposed to be assigned to her. I don't fuck with anything she or the other Crones have to say. I'm a smarter man than that."

"No shit," Luca whistled. "You're not going to give him a head's up?"

"Would *you* want me to tell you the Crones were meddling in your business?"

"Fuck no. They're about the only thing on this planet that scares me."

"Smart man. Do me a favor, swing by the client's apartment tonight. Just give it a once over in case her fiancé actually gives enough of a shit to have her covered. I'm betting you'll see that someone else is already there."

"Shit, he's gonna be pissed when he finds out," Luca said.

"When he finds out?"

"Yeah, that his life is about to change." Luca turned on his heel and marched out of the office.

King sighed and leaned back in his chair. His team were like his brothers. He never doubted that they would give their lives for him, and the same was true for him. He also dreaded getting a call from Ida. She was the Clan Rekkr's Crone, and when she called, you answered. Even the heads of their clans, the original families, never rejected a call from their Crones. They knew things. What they knew, and how they knew it was a mystery. They were a secretive old bunch. If they called and told you to be somewhere, you went. If they told you to accept a business deal, you did. They always had their clan's best interests at heart, and honestly, most people thought they were more like witches than wise matrons.

King also would do anything for his team even if they didn't want him to get involved. Pulling up his computer screen, King started doing an in-depth review of Charles Dillard III. He didn't think that this was going to be the last they heard of him if the Crone was so insistent that Van stay on the case.

CHAPTER 9

Cora wanted to look over at Van as he drove her home, but she didn't, because that would have been weird. She was worried Van was mad at her. It shouldn't matter if he was, she didn't know him. But it did matter; she didn't want him angry with her.

After a solid sobbing session she'd been dozing in the little room, waiting for something to happen, and he'd woken her up by barking at her, "We're leaving." She was startled because he was supposed to be finding her a ride. Then when he came back he seemed very put out that he was the one giving her that ride. She was going to remind him that she could take a car service but decided his current state wasn't one for suggestions.

Cora wasn't sure where they were going or why,

but she didn't think she was in any place to argue with him. They were heading away from the King Security office, which meant that she was being delivered to Chaz, who couldn't be bothered to come and collect her himself. Suddenly, it dawned on her. Maybe that was it; she needed to take to the highways and become a nomad. Cora Bridger, independent woman, traveling the country never stopping long enough to get tied down to anyone or anything. That was her last thought before she had to race to catch up to Van.

She had tried to follow him as he fast stepped out of the office. She managed to wave at Nadia, who smiled politely as they passed. They were down the elevator and into a flashy yellow car before she could ask him again where they were going.

"I'm taking you home."

Her heart skipped a beat. Not because she had wanted him to take her home. It skipped because she didn't have to see Chaz yet. She had a little more time before facing reality. This was the second moment of relief for the day. The first had been when she opened her eyes to see Van of Clan Rekkr looking down at her in that shitty warehouse.

"Thank you. I'm sure you have other things you could be doing."

He grunted at her. Cora was starting to think his grunts weren't that bad.

"Can I ask you a question?"

"You can ask, not sure I'll answer."

That would have deterred some people. Not her. "What kind of bear are you?"

She saw him twitch. Worried she might have overstepped herself, she tried to correct it. "I'm sorry. I shouldn't ask. I just think the Kindred are amazing. It must be so wonderful to be so strong, have a family that backs you up. It's different for us," she trailed off.

"For us?"

"Humans. We're a fickle bunch. Our relationships are so... flexible."

"Sometimes that's a good thing."

"It's not. It's like spending your life on a tightrope. Never knowing when you're going to fall."

"That's a bit dramatic."

Cora shrugged, not noticing that he hadn't answered her question. "So, did you talk to Chaz?"

"You know that's a stupid name, right? I mean who does that to a child?"

"His parents did. Too many Charles's in the family."

"That happens when you name your kids the

same name as yourself. I don't understand why humans do that."

"We don't have lineages like you do. Honestly, I think they started when paternity was still unsure and men wanted to try and cement their heirs."

"Still fucked up."

"Agreed." She waited for him to answer her.

"And to answer you, no. King called it in."

"King is your boss?"

"Boss, friend, clan member. We've known each since we were children. I was born into Rekkr. His family moved and was accepted in."

"I never understand how that works. Moving from one clan to another."

"No, you probably don't."

There was silence, so Cora chalked that up to another Kindred secret.

"So, your bear?"

"Grizzly, big and furry."

"That must be amazing," Cora sighed.

Van stopped at a light and turned to her. She glanced over and gasped. His eyes had gotten bigger, the gray color had given way to golden yellow and his face had spread wide. His teeth had lengthened and become sharp. His face was a morph between hand-some man and fierce predator.

"It's not bad," he said with a toothy smile.

Cora didn't know what happened next. She should have been scared of the man that had just casually showed her his animal while they were sitting at a stoplight. Instinct should have told her to jump out of the vehicle, even if it was still moving, to get away from the half man half beast next to her.

But that's not what she did.

She laughed.

It was a scream, mixed with hysterical laughter that startled even herself. He looked like a movie extra that had run away from the makeup department to sneak a cigarette.

Even with the long teeth and creepy eyes he was still ridiculously handsome. That thought made her laugh even harder. She grabbed her stomach as the tears fell down. Her blurry vision made her miss Van pulling over on the street and putting the car in park.

"I'm sorry, really," she wheezed. "You don't look bad. You look good really. I think I'm just tired, or emotional, I don't know," she said trying to get herself under control. Wiping at the tears that wouldn't stop falling. Clearly she was having some kind of mental break. Not that she didn't deserve one after her last few days. It didn't excuse her reaction. Poor Van must think she was a rude speciest or at least a bigot.

Taking a few deep breaths, she tried to pull it

together. Van wasn't looking at her. His face was back to his normal handsome self, but his eyes were trained on the back of the truck parked in front of them. His hands were on the steering wheel but his knuckles were white with the tightness of his grip, as though he was trying to bend the wheel into a new shape.

"Van? I'm sorry, I was just surprised. Really. I've never seen a Kindred mid-shift. It's actually amazing you can do that."

Van was silent and he was vibrating next to her. She could swear there were waves of energy pouring off him. The air in the car was suddenly intense and heavy.

Cora was starting to think she'd really screwed up. Shit, she was trapped in a car with an angry shifter. How the hell did she keep getting herself into these situations? It was like she was trying to win the world record for poor choices in one week.

"Do you want me to get out?" She didn't know what else to say to him at that point. She was guessing. The tension in the car made her want to bolt. But she also didn't want to wander the streets of Seattle wearing clothes that looked like she just skipped out on a court ordered rehab stay. Plus, there was the little problem of someone out to get her.

She reached for the door handle, but her fingers

had barely touched the surface before a growling roar punched through the quiet.

"Don't!"

Cora quickly snatched her hand back. The voice that came out of the man next to her was much more animal than human.

"Sorry," she whispered.

"Stop apologizing," he ground out.

"I'm..." she stopped herself before she did it again.

A minute ticked by, then another. She couldn't get out of the car, that much was clear. There wasn't anything she thought she could say that wouldn't make the situation worse. Not that she understood the situation at all. Maybe she should have just asked for music on the drive home and kept her mouth shut.

Who was she kidding, she would have talked over the music.

Van was next to her taking deep breaths. His eyes were closed but his hands were still on the wheel, squeezing the life out of it.

"Cora," he finally said, his eyes opening and turning to hers. His were bright yellow, his bear flashing between those animal eyes to the reflective Kindred eyes she had come to enjoy seeing.

She waited, she was learning.

"We have a situation."

Taking his words to mean that it was something to do with her kidnapping, she started urgently looking around. "Is someone following us?"

"No, you're safe, for now. I'm..." he paused shaking his body almost like an animal would. "I heard the call."

Confused even further, she wondered if he had an earpiece in or something.

"I didn't hear your phone? What kind of call? Was it Chaz?"

"Fuck Chaz!" he growled.

She wasn't going to deny that sentiment. Fuck Chaz for sure.

"Your boss?" she suggested, a little more timidly than she would have liked.

"The mating call."

That was about as far outside the possible responses she could have expected and her confusion made her blurt out, "What the fuck is a mating call?"

Van leaned closer to her, closing the space between them in the small car. "*My* mating call... *for you.*"

CHAPTER 10

Van couldn't hear anything but the roar of his blood crashing through his body. His skin was on fire, he could feel every follicle of hair standing on end as he fought to keep his body from shifting. His fucking bear wouldn't fit in his damn car, he was sure of that.

Cora had been bantering away next to him. When she spoke of her fascination with the Kindred he couldn't help but show off a little. Showing anyone a partial shift on purpose wasn't something he had ever done before. He done it in the heat of battle when adrenaline and anger fused together to allow him to unleash his other side, but this was different.

This was purely for her enjoyment and he

should have felt like a idiot for doing it. But the sheer joy on her face made it worth it. Until she started laughing. It was a tinkling sound that should have just been funny. He could have been mad she was laughing, assuming she thought he looked ridiculous.

Instead, that laugh, that sound of pleasure, turned into a song in his mind. It was as if an orchestra started playing his favorite song, if he had one. His heart seized at the sounds, his cock swelled right after that and he knew.

He just fucking knew.

She was his mate. *His. Fucking. Mate.*

He almost laughed. Almost. It was hilarious, really. A woman that he shouldn't have anything to do with once he dropped her off had instantaneously become the most important person in the world. At least to him.

"I need a minute. Don't move," he ordered while getting out of the car. He stalked over to the sidewalk and pulled out his phone.

It rang once before King picked up. "Talk."

The fucker always said "talk" when he answered the phone, as though everyone should assume he'd been waiting on them. Whatever.

"We have a problem."

"You have a tail?"

"You trying to be fucking funny?"

"Don't be an ass. Is there someone on you?"

"I sure as fuck wish there was. Different problem."

"I'm waiting."

"I heard it."

Van let that sit because he sure as hell didn't know how else to describe what just happened to him. They had been told since they were young that the mating call was different for everyone. It was unique and couldn't be explained except by those that had experienced it.

One thing was clear. Once the call was heard, there was never any doubt.

To reject it would be to tear out his own heart, and that scared the shit out of him.

"Heard it?"

"The call."

It was two words that to anyone else, any human, wouldn't have made any sense. But to one of the Kindred, it was a near sacred life experience.

There were moments to anticipate. Their first shift as a young person, the moment when puberty took over and your clan celebrated in a ceremony full of love and pride. The presentation of a clan knife, a talisman that would enable a Kindred to experience fast shifts in emergencies when getting tangled in clothes could harm or delay the process.

As an adult, these moments changed and took on more meaning. The moment that your clan acknowledged that you had a place amongst them by designating your first job. It was usually something menial, possibly cumbersome, but you did it out of respect and pride in your clan, and it wasn't done for any other reason than to prove your loyalty and deference to the clan leaders. Once it was done, and the elders were satisfied, your voice had weight, it had a place inside a group of people that treated each other as equals.

But the most important of these moments was the call. That moment that could be a touch, a feeling, even a taste that told you your soul mate was in front of you. Not every shifter would hear it, and some waited a long time for it... almost too long sometimes.

Her laugh was his call. Cora had been afraid, sad, angry, despondent, and a number of other emotions in the few hours since he'd met her. She'd had no reason to smile, or to laugh. Until he'd shown her part of his true self. He should find that upsetting, but he felt good that he had made her feel something good, even for a moment.

"Ida," King sighed.

"She knew." It was a statement, not a question.

"She was adamant that you be involved in this

case. I assumed it had something to do with the client, not the target. What do you need from me?" King wasn't about to questions how he knew, or even if he was sure. To do that would reject who and what they were.

"I don't fucking know." Van was pacing up and down the sidewalk. Humans and Kindred alike were giving him a wide berth. The emotions poured off him in waves that no one wanted to get caught up in.

"Does she know?"

"I told her, and then I got out of the car and she's sitting in there right now thinking who the hell knows what. She's staring at me through the window. What the hell do I do now? She's engaged. To an asshole, who for some reason I feel like gutting."

"I'd advise against that. This isn't the first time this has happened. Get her back to her apartment and I'll see who I can pull in to help you cover her. I'll also see if I can get her fiancé in to the office. I think we're going to need to have a face to face with him."

"Maybe I shouldn't be there for the first meeting."

Van knew that he wasn't going to be able to keep his hands away from anything he perceived as a threat to his mate. He also didn't even like the idea of having to leave her to deal with the ex. Because that was sure as hell what he was going to be. Her ex.

"Good call. I'll keep you updated."

"I want Luca on this, maybe Zion too if you can find him." Van trusted all of the men that made up their team, but he wanted those that had a slightly faster trigger finger to be the ones watching over his mate.

"I'll see what I can do."

The line clicked dead and Van shoved the phone back in his pocket. He looked over to see Cora looking down at her lap. She was frowning and he didn't like it.

He took a deep breath and looked up at the sky for a moment. He had to wonder why the Great Mother chose this way to unite souls. There had to be an easier, less shocking way. But then, why would anyone expect to find the love of their life in a quiet, non-emotional way? It was supposed to be shocking and life altering. So why would the creator do anything less fantastic than to hit you upside the head and throw your whole world upside down?

Stepping back around the car, he got in carefully and placed his hands back on the steering wheel.

"Sorry about that," he said with the briefest glance in Cora's direction. He didn't know if he could control himself enough to just look at her without appearing to want to eat her. He didn't want to scare her.

"About what? For dropping a bomb like that and then abandoning me? Or just for abandoning me? Because I don't know why you said what you did, but if it was supposed to be a joke, it was a bad one."

Turning to look at her, bracing himself for the impact of seeing his mate he said, "It wasn't a joke."

"Van, you can't say *mate* and *me* in the same sentence then walk away! Who does that?"

"I was surprised," he answered lamely.

"You think? I'm engaged in case you forgot."

"I didn't forget, but that's over."

"Because you say it is?"

"Yeah, because he's a dick and I'm your mate."

"You can't just *say* that!"

"I can because it's the truth. I'm your mate. You're mine and that isn't going to change."

"I'm really sorry. I can't imagine what this means for you, but I have my own shit to deal with right now."

"I'm here to help you with that shit."

"It's not shit, it's my life, Van! My messy, confusing life. I have to figure out Chaz. I have to decide my next steps. That doesn't include... whatever you're offering. I don't even know what you're offering. The Kindred don't exactly put out a manual on this for humans."

"It's private, secret."

"Well, good for you. For us it's just an unknown and for me, right now, it's another bucket of preverbal shit that I have to haul around."

Van didn't like her calling it that. It pissed him off. Not at her. No, she was allowed to feel whatever she wanted. She could be angry at him for his revelation but it wouldn't change how he felt. But his anger was tenfold at the fact she had been held captive for almost a week. She'd been mistreated and the man that was supposed to be protecting her had all but ignored her and then hired someone else to find her. Where was he?

"I don't want you to worry about that."

"Please don't tell me what you want me to worry about. I get to decide that. And right now, I don't want to worry about this. I want to go home and order a bunch of pizza, Hawaiian or all meat, I could use the protein, and maybe some Thai food and get really drunk. That's what I want to do. I really don't care what *you* or any other man wants from me right now."

Van didn't want that. He wanted to take her back to his loft. He wanted to kill anyone that was threatening her and he wanted her naked and in his bed.

"I can get those things for you. I don't want to just leave you back at your place. It's not secure. I have security, and I know my place is safe."

Cora started tapping her chin. "Wow, that seems reasonable. Our relationship has hit that crucial point. You know the three-hour point that says I should move in with you. What is the traditional gift for a three-hour anniversary? Wood or plastic? Maybe nothing, because there is *no such thing*!" She yelled the last words and Van gritted his teeth and wished that she wasn't upset. Wishing wasn't going to help.

"This is important. This is our life together."

"We don't *have* a life together. I'm not ignorant. I know that Kindred mate for life. But that can't be me. It certainly can't be you."

"Why not me?"

"Because... you're big. And kinda mean. And you never smile. Oh, wait, and the fact that I don't freaking know you!"

"Doesn't change anything."

"Actually, it changes everything. Those reasons are the ones that are going to make you take me to my apartment or I'm going to get out and walk there myself. Your choice."

"I don't want you at your place."

"That's too fucking bad, Van. I want to go home."

Van started the car and pulled out into traffic quickly, cutting off more than one car.

"If you don't mind. I'd like to get there alive," she said crossing her arms.

"Like I would let anything happen to you."

"Like I would know that or even assume that. You did your job, Van. No more kidnappers, I'm back. Deal is done. Move on."

"There is no moving on. There is only us."

He heard her make a tiny growling sound and almost smiled. Now wasn't the time. There was too much in the air. Too much confusion, too much desire, at least coming from him. He was having trouble keeping his mind on the road when all it wanted to think about was having her under him. The urge to mark her, plant himself deep inside her and make her his was almost a painful feeling.

There was so much more that needed to happen before that. It was a sad fact that made his skin crawl. His confusion with his physical body craving her and his desire to protect her from harm seemed to be conflicting.

He had to figure out what he could control and

what he couldn't. At the moment he needed to provide a safe space and food for his mate.

Hitting a button on the steering wheel he spoke aloud to call the office. Nadia answered.

"Nadia, I need two pizzas delivered to Ms. Butler's address. One all meat, and one with that pineapple crap on it. Also order Thai from somewhere nice. Get an assortment. Then have a few bottles of wine delivered also. Put it on my personal account."

"Done," Nadia said, hanging up.

"I'm sorry, did you just... I don't know what that was, micromanage my evening?"

"Micromanage?"

"Well, you took over."

"I didn't take over. You said you needed something. I took care of it. It's what I'm going to be doing from now on."

"I don't need you to take care of anything. I need you to..."

"To what?"

"To drive. You can drop me off at the front door. I'll get Joe to let me in."

"Joe?"

"The building manager... it's fine..."

"No."

"Excuse me?"

"No. I'll be walking you up, checking your apartment and then having dinner with you."

"No. You. Are. Not! I'm going home, Van. *My* home, not yours."

"Same thing now."

"Grr, you're so frustrating!"

"Grr isn't a word."

"It is when I'm dealing with *you*. You know I could just call the police."

"But you won't."

"Screw you, maybe I will." She was huffing and sputtering very unconvincingly.

"You've had enough drama today. You need to relax."

Cora laughed. "And you think you're helping? News flash, you're not. In fact, I'm very unrelaxed."

"Give me time."

CHAPTER 11

What the hell was she going to do now? Cora's frustration and anger was struggling to keep up with her exhaustion, but the exhaustion was winning.

Van had lost his mind. Maybe it was the stress of her rescue, or that he regretted beating up those idiots. Maybe if he spent a little more time with her he'd realize that there was some kind of mix up.

She was less than the ideal Kindred mate. She hadn't worked in years. True, she was part of a number of boards and committees, but those were all focused on helping the Dillard family with their business connections. She liked to volunteer, it gave her a purpose and even though the face of the events were mostly focused on rich people being rich, they did raise money for good causes.

Cora also didn't think that she was any great beauty. She never thought of herself as ugly. But to her, mated Kindred couples always had some kind of aura around them. They always looked beautiful and content. There was no way that she could measure up to the women in the the couples she'd seen, especially standing next to Van.

And most importantly, she was already engaged to Chaz who fucking hated the Kindred. It was going to be bad enough breaking up with him without a hulking bear shifter looming over her shoulder as she told her fiancé that he'd been replaced.

Oh god, that picture popped into her mind and she wanted to chuck herself straight out of the car.

Maybe when she fell asleep tonight she would wake up and it would all be a dream. Not that she wanted to be back in that warehouse tied to that stupid pole in a nasty room. But compared with her current predicament, it was starting to look appealing.

Van pulled up to her building and with a quick, "Stay here," he got out and walked up to the doorman speaking to him briefly and then shaking his hand.

He came over to her door and opened it.

"Come on," he instructed.

"Van, this isn't a parking spot. My car is in mine so you are going to have to park somewhere else."

This would also give her a chance to barricade herself in her apartment away from him.

"Evan here is going to be nice enough to watch my car until backup gets here and can move it for me."

He cupped her elbow and started walking her towards the door. Evan the traitor opened it and touched the brim of his hat as they passed.

She smiled at him grimly, it wasn't his fault that Van was a manipulative butthead.

They walked to the elevators and Van hit the button, his hand still cupping her elbow. She didn't resist the walk to the elevator because she didn't want to cause a scene. She'd had enough of those.

The doors opened and they stepped in. She didn't need to tell Van the floor number because apparently he knew everything. He hit the button for the eighth floor.

"You can just drop me off, you know."

"I already told you, no. For a number of reasons. First, you don't have a key."

"Shit, I'm going to have to call the motel and see if they have my purse. It's probably empty, but still."

"I'll take care of that tomorrow. Evan is calling

the super to meet us up here. After that we have dinner coming."

She wanted to argue, Lord knew she did. But every word she spoke was making her body ache. She was so tired that she wanted to cry. She really didn't know how much fight she had left in her.

They reached her floor and stepped out. By the time they got to her door, Joe the building manager was running towards them a big smile on his face.

Cora couldn't remember him ever being that excited to help a tenant.

"I've got your key right here, Ms. Butler," he said and opened her door and threw his arm wide in a welcoming gesture as though she were royalty about to enter her palace.

Cora shrugged and walked into the apartment, flipping on the light switch by the kitchen as Van handed the eager building manager a few bills for his trouble.

The apartment had been Dillard approved. It was a two-bedroom two-bath layout. Not grandiose but respectable. The floor to ceiling windows in the living room looked out over the city, and she loved this view, especially at night. Chaz had let her buy whatever she wanted, and she'd decorated in creams and blues. A long L-shaped sofa was a soft taupe color but sat atop a bright turquoise rug. The TV opposite it was large enough to see but not take over the whole room. Cora had added things that made her happy. A piece of driftwood she had found at the beach. A curving glass sculpture made by a local artist that had been selling their wares at a local craft market a few years ago. Anything to give the space a little life and remove the sanitary stamp Chaz had issued when she moved in.

Inside the kitchen she pulled open a drawer, grabbed a corkscrew, and then retrieved a bottle of wine from her fridge. She had it open and was pouring herself a large glass before she ever looked back at Van.

"You drinking?"

"No. How much are you going to drink?"

"Oh-ho-ho, don't even go there, mister. You are in *my* house *without* my invitation. I'm going to do what I want. I don't need your approval. In fact, I don't need *any* man telling me how much wine I should drink after a traumatic experience. You do remember the traumatic experience, right? The one where I was tied up against my will for days on end while being tormented by two idiots... I was scared and miserable, remember? I think that deserves more than a measly thimble full of wine. I plan on getting trashed tonight. I want to be so numb that I can't feel how sore my face is or wonder how much time I'm going to have to spend with my chiropractor to fix my shoulders. I want to let my mind go fuzzy and sleep for at least twelve hours."

Topping off her wine she walked over to the couch and set down her drink before flopping onto it. She really wanted to fight with Van. She wanted to kick him out and be alone.

But that was a lie.

She didn't want to be alone. The thought terrified her, but she also knew that telling him that would only cement him into her space. From what he'd said in the car, there would be no getting rid of him anyway, but there was no sense making him feel like she really wanted him there. That she needed him to be there.

Van moved through her apartment methodically, going into each room. He started on the left side, walking down the small hallway turning on all the lights. He disappeared into the spare room that she used as an office, and then she heard the shower curtain open and close in the bathroom. He continued his survey, moving past the living room to the other side of the apartment, which was her master bedroom. She heard the patio door open in her bedroom then close. He never asked for permission. Logic said he was checking for boogeymen. Or he could be pillaging her underwear drawer, who knew?

He came back around to the front room, walking past her to look down the windows as though he was checking for Spider-Man on the side of the building.

"Anyone shimmying up the glass that I should know about?"

He glanced back at her, his eyes flashing with that silver reflection. "Nobody yet."

"Okay then, you let me know if you start seeing wings or webs out there. I'll get my emergency home defense weapon."

"Pepper spray?"

"No, my Lacrosse stick, I played in high school."

She could almost see the humor in it. But she was too tired to laugh.

The doorbell rang and Van went into alert mode. He approached the door and looked through the peephole.

He opened it just enough to complete the transaction and came back with the pizza Nadia had ordered. Once it was on the counter, the bell rang again and he returned this time with a number of take-out bags.

Cora figured she should probably go in and help because he wouldn't know where anything was. But then she remembered that she wasn't helping him invade her space. Although she could smell the pizza and it was making her mouth water.

Her stomach had handled the sandwich from earlier and it was growling for more.

Van came back from the kitchen with two plates, some napkins, and the take-out bags, setting everything on the coffee table. He went back and returned with two pizza boxes and a bottle of wine under his arm.

He sat down next to her, close enough that her feet were touching his thick thigh when she pulled them up on the cushion.

She watched as he organized the coffee table as though he'd come over to her house and had dinner with her a million times. Which was crazy, because she didn't even think Chaz had even eaten at her apartment before. They'd met up and gone out for food and he occasionally stayed over, but he preferred her to stay overnights at his place because he would work at odd hours and needed his computers.

Van handed her a plate and fork and Cora closed her eyes and sniffed. Pad Thai and drunken noodles. Normally she'd pick one or the other, but right now, a pile of greasy noodles sounded amazing and she'd never turn down hot food. Especially when it smelled this good.

Forking a huge bite of noodles into her mouth, she moaned happily. Van's eyes shot to her face, his eyes flashing yellow before cooling back to the silver gray.

"Sorry, it's good."

"I'm glad," he said huskily.

Van started eating too, pausing to look at his phone and only putting down his plate to text something quickly then pick his fork back up.

"Working?" It was obvious, but she just wanted to cover up some of the sounds of her slurping her noodles.

"Arranging your detail."

"My detail?"

"In the event I'm not available, I need to know who is going to be covering you."

Shaking her head, she said again, "Covering me?"

Van opened a box of pizza and pulled out a slice covered in ham and pineapple, he unceremoniously dropped it on the tiny bare section of her plate. "Eat."

"I am. What are you talking about?" She absentmindedly picked up the pizza and started eating it. Hawaiian might not be everybody's favorite, but it sure as hell was hers.

"Your ex hasn't arranged for any kind of bodyguard for you. I'm now your bodyguard. If I'm unavailable or need to be somewhere, I'll have one of the other guys on you."

"I don't want anyone on me!" She hated the way that sounded, but she'd said it now.

"We haven't resolved who kidnapped you, or why. Your ex should have been handling it, but he didn't. Now it's my job."

"No, it's not. It's totally Chaz's problem. I was kidnapped because of him. It's not like I'm some dignitary or something. Obviously this was some retaliation against him. I'm going to dump him so I won't be a target any longer. And stop calling him my ex."

"He *is* your ex, because I'm your now."

"You are not. You are... a persistent employee," she grumbled.

"No, I'm your mate. I'm going to be your body-guard, best friend, lover, partner, and everything else in between."

"Oh geez, how will that ever fit on your business card?" she mocked.

"Go ahead and sass, it doesn't bother me. You have a free pass after the bullshit you went through. But I'm here and I'm staying."

"Did it ever occur to you that I don't feel the same? I just met you, and it wasn't over cocktails at a charity fundraiser to save the whales. You dragged me out of a hellhole. You think that sets us up for a future of happiness? How do you even know what I'm looking for in a man? I'm still in a long-term relationship that I'm *thinking* of getting out of. Who in their right mind would jump into another relationship without taking a time-out to reassess their life choices?"

"Easy, that's what humans do. I'm not human. Kindred mate for life. That means there is nothing more important to us than finding our mates and making them happy. The survival of our species demands it. We don't even have a choice. We hear the call and it's as if our DNA re-sequences to merge with yours. All we care about is our mates. Your safety and happiness are my only priorities. I'm not worried about what kind of man you want, but I'll be whatever kind of man you need. So as far as you're concerned, I'm every possibility."

"I've always wanted a million boyfriends," she said sarcastically.

Van shrugged. "Did you know that as the Kindred age without a mate, we no longer seek out sexual partners?"

"Ahh, performance issues," she whispered loudly.

"No, that's never a problem. We can't actually

stand to have anyone touch us. Our animal nature rejects it. We don't want anyone's scent on us that isn't our mate's. When someone touches us accidently it feels like a violation."

"So, earlier, when I touched you. Did it bother you because you hadn't heard the call?"

"No, it didn't. It felt good. I haven't felt anything like that in so long. I didn't understand, but it was because you were meant to be mine."

Cora kind of liked that. It was sweet. He didn't want to vomit when she touched him. That was a great start.

"Are you saying it's been a while for you? You know, getting any?"

Van laughed, his straight white teeth flashing at her. "Yes, it's been a while."

"Huh, and you're saying that you're interested in me that way?"

Those silver eyes flashed again. "Oh, I'm more than interested, Cora. In fact, I've been trying to figure out how much recovery time you might need before we can get to that."

"How about three years? That work for you?" That wasn't far off what she was thinking. Not that she didn't find Van sexy. The man was incredibly fuckable. It had been a while, but she wasn't able to ignore that. In fact, she could easily say he had affected her from the moment she got a clear view of his eyes. His sexuality was potent; she could feel it coming off him.

She shouldn't be thinking about Van like that. Technically, she was still in a relationship. Granted it was a broken one that needed to be severed permanently. To be honest, Chaz rarely did it for her. He was cute, not what she would call handsome. In college he had those perfect frat boy looks. Four years later, he still looked the same, except that frat boy had evolved into more of a 'playboy douche' look. He spent more time on his hair than she did. He tanned weekly and had facials monthly.

He didn't go to clubs unless he knew there was a VIP section and that he was going to be sitting in it. During family dinners his father would scold him for running up bar tabs in the fifty thousand dollar range. How anyone spent that much money on booze was a mystery to Cora. The only times they'd been intimate in the last few years were when they'd both drunk too much. It was as unpleasant as it sounded.

Van was right about one thing. No matter how sexy he was, she couldn't even imagine that at the moment.

She was waiting for Van to respond to her three year comment when the doorbell rang again. Van got up to answer it. He checked the peephole before opening the door and stepping back. Two hulking men entered the room. Their eyes went straight to her and she leaned over to set her plate down.

Van stepped in front of them, and then stood to the side as he introduced them.

"Babe, this is Anson and Luca. If I'm not around, they will be."

Cora looked to the two men. The first one he called Anson was drop dead gorgeous. Like almost too pretty. He had shoulder-length brown hair that was the same color as his short-cropped beard. His skin was tanned and it made his bright blue eyes shine before they flashed silver at her.

The other man, Luca, looked to be Latino in heritage with burnished skin and graceful bone structure. He had black hair and mean looking frown.

"Don't call me babe. I don't need a 'detail,'" she said making air quotes with her fingers as she said the last word.

"What's wrong with calling you babe?"

"You don't know me, that's what. My name is Cora. Hell, even Ms. Butler is better. You call someone 'babe' when you can't remember their name."

"Hmm, how about baby?"

She didn't want to admit it didn't bother her as

much when he said it. "You're not winning any points here, ace. Like I said, I don't need a babysitter."

"With all due respect, ma'am," started Anson. "It looks like the men that took you were working for someone else. That someone else might have connection with one of the local crime syndicates. Specifically the Kristanzi family."

"So that still doesn't mean it had anything to do with me."

"No, it means that your ex is up to something he shouldn't be. I know that the Dillard family doesn't always keep its nose clean when it comes to business, but getting involved with the Ukrainians is never a good idea."

"Ukrainians?" she asked confused.

"Yes, ma'am. They tend to run drugs, guns, and do a steady business loan sharking," Anson explained.

"Why would Chaz be doing business with them in the first place? Does his father know about this?" Cora was shocked. Chaz's father was usually the picture of caution when it came to his business alliances, and she couldn't believe that he would approve of anything like this. Unless this was something that he wanted to keep hidden. She wouldn't put it past Charles Dillard the second to be into something shady if no one would find out about it. Especially his wife.

"That's what we need to figure out. If those two idiots were working under the Kristanzi family than there's something your ex isn't telling you."

"Stop calling him my ex," she ground out.

The man named Luca didn't smile, but his eyes squinted as though he might. She waited, but his expression never changed. Cora decided that he was a scary motherfucker.

"Yeah, all this 'security,'" she said making her air quotes again. "Chaz isn't going to pay for it. It wouldn't be cost effective. That's why I knew he'd never pay that ransom. Chaz Dillard isn't going to part with a million dollars for me."

Van made a low noise in his throat. "Why wouldn't he?"

She shook her head sadly. "Because the Dillards know when to cut their losses."

Cora didn't have much to say after that. The cameras seemed to be a waste. Her building had never felt unsafe, but maybe Van saw things differently. It wasn't a fight she wanted to put much effort into at the moment. All she wanted to do was cry herself to sleep. She was full and her emotions were starting to bubble up. She felt the first tear fall down her cheek. Van cleared his throat.

"I'll keep in touch with you both. After you have the cameras set up, figure out a rotating shift. I'll take one too to cover the front. I just want eyes on anyone out of the ordinary. If they try to grab her from here they're either stupid or desperate."

Van was saying this to the other two men, but Cora didn't bother to include herself. She heard them leave and then she was lifted off the couch by Van before she could even squeak in protest.

"Bed."

"Van, didn't you hear what I said? I can't afford security, hell, I'm not sure I can afford Top Ramen."

"I did. I'm paying for your safety. I'll put a hundred cameras up if that's what it takes. The guys aren't charging me to watch you. They know I'd do it for them if they needed it. You are important, and not just to me. Keeping you out of harm is worth any money, any effort. Now, you're going to bed. I'm going to clean up, and then I'm staying the night in case you need me." He set her by the bathroom door in her room and gave her a little shove. She shook her head and then went into the bathroom.

Cora took a moment to stare at her reflection. The bedraggled woman staring back at her was almost unrecognizable. Her cheek had turned a lovely purple shade, the edge of her eye was puffy but she could blink without it hurting. Her lip had cracked open again from eating. It stung so she dug into a drawer and found some ointment and slathered it on. Still wearing her King Security loaner clothes, and she couldn't be bothered to change out of them.

Opening the door she found Van right where she left him. She started to walk to the bed, and he took two quick steps and picked her up again.

"Will you please put me down!"

He didn't answer, instead he put her down on her bed. He'd pulled back the covers while she'd been in the bathroom. She wanted to be angry at him, but the sheets just felt so goddamn good.

"Oh, man," she moaned, pushing the unbruised side of her face into the pillow. It was like someone turned off a switch. There was still a hulking handsome man in her room that she barely knew and she couldn't even open her eyes to even tell him to leave.

"Sleep, I'm here," he said quietly and kissed her on the forehead. She felt the covers being pulled over her and her last thought was how nice it was to have someone care about her. Even a little bit.

CHAPTER 12

Van waited for Cora to fall asleep. He stood over her, watching the slow rise and fall of her chest as she breathed. He needed to know she was okay. There was no safer place for her than under his eye. He knew she didn't like that, but it was a simple fact.

King had been sending him information as he got it. The two men who had taken Cora from her hotel room had been identified, they were known lackeys of the Kristanzi family. Hangers on who were used occasionally for jobs that had a high probability of getting caught. That often meant that there was something much bigger going down. It was an excellent cover as the hired parties went through anonymous sources to get their jobs and often took them without being paid first.

Both men had been dumb enough to show up at a local emergency room and King had called in a tip to a few friends he had at the Seattle Police Department. Both were wanted under multiple warrants and were arrested immediately. They would be recovering at the local jail until their trials.

Van knew that he wasn't going to be able to watch Cora twenty-four-seven, but he also wasn't sure if he was going to be able to leave her anytime soon.

Deciding to let her rest, he stepped out of her room and pulled the door closed leaving a crack open.

Anson and Luca were setting up across the street at an office building that had a vacant space. They were borrowing it he believed. Borrowing being a loose term. Her building wasn't wholly without security, but it wasn't like his loft. The guys had put up some temporary cameras that were being fed to them and back to the offices.

The last text he got was that King had made the call to Mr. Dillard and he was going to be heading over to Cora's house after he was done with work.

That would give Van enough time to clean up and try very hard to tamp down his rage. That fuckwad had been told his girl was safe and he was going to visit her after work? Van wasn't naïve, King would have told him that she was safe and healthy and that a member of staff was returning her to her home. But to Van, it didn't excuse the lack of urgency.

Van was standing in the kitchen taking deep breaths, keeping his animal down. He almost wanted to talk to someone about how he was feeling, but he wasn't known for calling up one of the guys for a chat.

Instead, he pulled out his phone and went over the information King had sent again. Every new revelation made him more worried and more adamant that he was responsible for her safety.

In the morning he was going to install a new security system inside her apartment. He wasn't stupid enough to think that he could drag her off to his loft, so he needed to make sure that when she was at home, there was more than one set of eyes on it.

He heard a knock and braced himself. He went to the door and looked through and saw King's mug way too close to the door. Opening it, he immediately smelled another human and stepped into King's space forcing him back. Van closed the door behind him and stood in front of it with his arms folded over his chest.

"King."

"Van, I'd like you to meet Charles Dillard III. He's here to see Cora."

Van looked past King to the man standing behind him. Charles Dillard III was probably five-foot-ten and was dressed like he was on his way to a boat launch. His khaki pants and polo shirt with a popped collar made Van hate him just a little bit more than he already did. He let his eyes travel down the man and saw he wasn't wearing socks and his shoes looked like they cost more than most people's monthly salary. In other words, he looked like an absolute preppy douchebag.

"Cora's sleeping."

"Well, big guy," Chaz said, his voice was weak and annoying. At least to Van's ears. "I'm sure she won't mind me waking her up."

"If you wanted to see her after she's been missing for a week, maybe you should have come over sooner. Waking her up now would not benefit her in any way."

Chaz looked at him with shock then he started laughing as if Van had just told the best joke he'd ever heard. "Hey, I get it, you guys are good at your job. But I'm here to see *my fiancée*. I'm sure she would like to see me. Now, if you don't mind," he said, starting to step past Van.

Van blocked him, easily covering the door with his large frame. "I *do* mind. Cora was injured by her captors. She's dehydrated and starved. She doesn't need you to wake her from the healing sleep she is in so you can, I don't know, tell her about your week?"

"Hey! It doesn't really matter *why* I want to wake her up. She's my fiancée and I'll do what I want."

"Why didn't you try to find her?" Van asked, not bothering to tell the man she wasn't his fiancée anymore.

"I did, I called *you* guys. And look, you found her! Mission accomplished. Now get out of my way!" Chaz was starting to turn an interesting shade of red. If he was trying to intimidate Van or King, he was failing.

"I'm sorry, I can't do that. Cora is my responsibility. I have to do what is in her best interest," Van explained.

Chaz turned to King, "Look, I understand that you guys are a full-service operation, but this is ridiculous. I want to see Cora. Tell him to move."

King was leaning casually against the opposite wall. "Mr. Dillard, the situation with Cora has changed. I'm afraid I'm not going to be able to make him move."

"What the fuck is going on here! I want to see

my fiancée!" Chaz screeched, his voice rising shockingly high.

"See, Chaz, that's the problem. She's not your woman anymore," Van said firmly. He took a small amount of enjoyment out of saying those words. He also let his eyes flash at the little wiener of a man just to remind him that he wasn't dealing with anyone less than a Kindred.

"What the fuck is that supposed to mean?" The man seemed to be shrinking in front of Van's eyes.

"See the reason it took so long for you to get a ransom call was because she had run away from you. That's right, she hightailed it out of a dress fitting, still wearing the gown mind you, and holed up in a local motel. She was there for two days trying to come to terms with the fact that she didn't want to be with you anymore. Then she was kidnapped and held hostage. Imagine her horror that the man she was supposed to marry wasn't even looking for her, let alone worried about where she went."

"I *was* worried! You don't know Cora. She flakes out and disappears all the time. She won't answer my calls, and then she leaves me vague messages and acts all passive aggressive for a few days before she comes to her senses. It's not my fault she got herself kidnapped!"

That was the wrong thing to say. Van felt his

canines dropping as he took a step closer to the man. "You might want to rethink that. Nobody, and I mean *nobody* just 'gets themselves kidnapped.' The men that took her knew where she was. They've been hired through various channels by the Kristanzi family in the past, never knowing who they were working for. That name sound familiar?"

The whiny man paled just a little. *Bullseye.*

"It seems logical to assume that these men were hired to kidnap Cora and extort money from you. Did you ignore their message? Or did you know that you couldn't pay back whatever you owed? Not to mention the asshole tax they tacked on to that ransom demand."

"I don't know anything," he stammered.

"Well, I'm glad to hear it. Because anyone that owes money to that family usually ends up paying in one way or another. I'm not going to let Cora be used as leverage for something someone else fucked up." Van said this with a growl at the end.

King broke in at that point with a quiet reminder. "No shifting here, Van."

Van knew he couldn't shift in the hallway. It was dangerous for everyone having a huge bear taking up a small space. But he wasn't going to let the opportunity pass to make sure Chaz understood him.

"What's it to you? I mean, we're getting married

in a few weeks. She's just got cold feet. And I'm sure whatever this kidnapping business is will resolve itself." Chaz was desperately trying to sound confident, but he was failing. Badly.

"First off, Cora doesn't have cold feet. She told me she doesn't care about you and that she's pretty sure you don't care about her. Second, she wants a different life than the one she has, and I'm going to make sure she gets that. And finally, Cora is my mate. If you think for one second I'm going to leave her with you so that you can get her killed with your negligence, you're as stupid as you look."

Van knew that his fangs were showing, but he couldn't bring himself to pull them back. He smelled fear in the man in front of him. He was weak. Van couldn't stand weakness. How Cora had stayed with him this long was shocking. Cora was strong. She was fierce. Even after being held captive by a couple of idiots for a week she was still all sass and attitude. This tiny man would be crying for his mommy after half a day of what Cora had been through.

"Your *mate*? How can she be your mate? She's going to be my wife!"

"That's where you're wrong. She's mine and I've already told her."

"And what, she's just going along with it?"

Van laughed at the man. "If you really think

Cora just accepted that, then you don't know her at all. As of right now, she's no longer your concern. When she's ready to talk to you we'll arrange a time and place for the two of you two meet. Somewhere public and I'll be present."

"This is fucking ridiculous!" Chaz spat. Turning to King he tried another tactic. "Is this how you run your business? Do you make a habit of stealing your client's wives?"

"If she was that easy to steal, was she ever really yours?" King asked casually.

Van wasn't sure how he did it, but King could always cut someone to the quick with an accurate, if not brutal observation.

Chaz realized he wasn't going to win against the men in the hallway and he started backing up. "This isn't over. I'm going to tell everyone I know not to work with you. I can ruin you!" Chaz was saying this while he was still retreating down the hall. He wasn't very threatening.

King took a step towards the man. "You know, Mr. Dillard. Chaz. I'm not really concerned about that. Anyone you work with, well, let's just say they aren't in the same class as our clientele. I'm sorry for the inconvenience. I'm sure you'll come to understand that this is the best course of action for all parties."

"Fuck you, and fuck *you!*" Chaz hissed, tossing up a middle finger at both King and Van.

They watched him enter the elevator and waited a moment for the doors to close.

"I think that went well," King said casually as he turned to Van.

"I wanted to rip that little fucker's head off. What a dick. He didn't even push the issue about seeing her."

"Well, you *were* blocking the door. He didn't really have a chance."

"If someone was standing between you and your woman, wouldn't you want to tear him to pieces to get to her?"

King shook his head. "I'd like to think that I would. I'm not sure what you're feeling, so I'm going to have to assume the right answer is yes."

"She's exhausted. She fell asleep the second her head hit the pillow. She was too tired to even fight with me, and based on our brief encounters, I think it might be her favorite thing to do."

"I'm sure we haven't heard the last of Mr. Charles Dillard III."

"Fuck him. Like I care if he's going to bad mouth us. We have a reputation that no little punk like him could harm. But I'm pretty sure that that sickly white color he turned when I mentioned the Kristanzis doesn't bode well. I have to wonder if his father knows anything about it. Cora said something about his father being a careful businessman... at least on the surface."

King rubbed his chin. "So, tattle on him to his father? See what shakes loose?"

"No, not yet. If he had the means to resolve this before he would have. I don't think his father is going to help him out of this hole."

King nodded. "I have a call with Ida at five thirty tomorrow. I'll see if she has any further insight."

"She called you, didn't she?"

"She did, she's been checking in. I'm sorry, man. I didn't know why she wanted you on this case, just that she did. Would you have wanted me to tell you?"

"No, I mean I wouldn't change what I've been given for anything. Knowing about it wouldn't have made a difference."

"You seem to have settled in awful quick. I can't imagine that change being an easy one. One moment a confirmed bachelor, the next...."

"It's only been two hours, and I feel like I've lived a whole other lifetime. I can hear her in the other room breathing. Second to the mating call, it's the sweetest fucking sound I've ever heard in my life."

"I'm happy for you, man. Cora's special. I mean, she'd have to be for the creator to pick her for you, right? Just remember that she's had a shit time, so be careful," King said. He wasn't saying that because Van wasn't aware of the fragility of the situation. He was saying it because sometimes a friend had to let you know that he understood your challenges.

"She's so fragile right now. That sad sack of human has taken any sense of pride she had and wiped it away. And he did it by ignoring her. How in the fuck do you ignore a woman as beautiful and funny as Cora?"

King slapped him on the shoulder. "The fact that you think that traumatized woman who seems to be surviving on sarcasm is funny tells me everything I need to know. Anson and Luca filled me in on their little encounter with her. By the way, they like her for you too. Even Luca said she was a suitable mate."

"Suitable. That's high praise from him. I appreciate you coming down with that piece of work. There was a good chance I wouldn't have been able to control myself if I'd been on my own."

"I figured. You're a strong shifter and you use your animal to defend those that need defending. Cora Butler needs you whether she realizes it or not. I'll call in help if I need it. You keep an eye on your mate, and if you're smart, you'll call Ida and thank her."

"Thank her?" Van thought that was a weird idea.

"Trust me. You always want to be on the Crone's good side. Ida is partial to chocolates and PBS. That woman will give you lottery numbers if you work it right," King said, and Van was pretty sure that he was only partially joking.

Van shook his head. "This is a whole new world for me. Crones and mates then what?"

"I think it goes claiming, marriage, and then cubs. Congratulations, Van."

King gave Van a one-armed hug and walked down the hallway. Van let himself back into Cora's apartment and secured the door. Turning off the lights, he entered her room and shucked off his clothes. He set his gun and phone on the nightstand nearest the patio door. Slipping into the bed, he did his best not to disturb her as he pulled her into his arms. She didn't protest, her body was limp. Van brought her head to his chest and made sure she was tucked tightly against him.

Nobody was going to hurt Cora Butler. Not while he was still breathing.

CHAPTER 13

Cora was warm. It had to be a dream, because she hadn't been physically warm in more than a week. She hadn't gotten used to the cold, but it had become a constant companion of sorts.

She wasn't cold now, so her mind must be trying to salvage her sanity during her ordeal. She was comfortable, and there was something soft underneath her and something hard and even warmer next to her. Not wanting to wake up to the reality of her existence in the cold warehouse she snuggled her face into the block of heat next to her.

There was a manly scent in her heater. It was like soap and sleep, if that had a scent, and it was a very nice dream that she didn't want to wake up from. Her eyes were closed and she kept them that way for fear of breaking the spell.

Burrowing deeper she felt the wall of heat slither around her. It pulled her tighter to itself. That was nice. She really hoped that when she woke up, she would remember this feeling. She felt safe. That's how she knew it had to be a dream. That wasn't a feeling she usually ever associated with herself. Safe was for people that had their shit together. That wasn't her.

Cora's wall of heat moved again, this time coming in contact with her ass. That was strange, walls weren't usually known to be grabby. But it felt nice. The wall hand was rubbing her butt and it made her want to purr. That hand moved up and down her back, then down to the back of her thigh hiking it up over something. That felt good too.

Then she felt a kiss. A warm, soft kiss on her neck. Okay now things were getting freaky. She was being molested by a wall? What kind of wall was this?

Not that it didn't feel good, because, oh boy, did it. She arched her neck giving the lips more room to maneuver.

In response to her movement, the kiss turned more heated. Then she felt it, the slight scrape of something sharp.

Her eyes flew open and she was face to face with Van.

"Van, what the hell?"

"Good morning," he said, his voice rough and growly.

"Why are you in my bed?"

"I was bodyguarding, your body to be precise."

"You can't just jump into bed with me!"

"Funny, because I did. You slept in my arms all night."

"That's because I didn't know it was you! I thought it was a warm wall!" She knew that sounded crazy but her mind wasn't exactly firing on all its cylinders yet.

"Warm wall?"

"Yes, a warm cozy wall that was the opposite of that stupid freezing room I've been in," she grumped.

She wasn't unaware she was still wrapped in his arms, her leg hiked up over his. It would have been an awkward position if she hadn't been so damn comfortable.

"I'm sorry you had to go through that, sweets. I'm sorry I wasn't there to protect you," he said. His eyes scanning over her face as he tucked a strand of hair behind her ear.

"You didn't know me," she whispered back.

"Doesn't matter. I'm going to feel that shit. You

were in this town, being hurt and abused, and I wasn't there to take care of you. Doesn't matter that I didn't know you yet. I still feel it. I wish we could have met last week. I wish I'd met you at a coffee shop, heard you laugh at something you were reading. You could have avoided all this pain."

Shit, that was really nice. A little weird, but still nice. "Van that's crazy."

"Maybe, but there it is."

Cora wasn't sure what to say next. She was pondering that when she remembered the heat of his mouth against her neck and her hand flew to touch the side of her throat. "Did you give me a hickey?"

A slow grin spread across his handsome face. "Maybe."

"You fucker! Why did you do that?"

"Because, I don't think I'm going to be able to fuck you for a few days and I wanted to make sure something of me was marking you."

"Fuck me? Have you lost your mind? I'm engaged!"

"Not anymore."

"Well, you might feel that way, but I need to have a conversation with Chaz about that."

"I already did."

Cora pushed herself out of his arms to lean away from him. "You what?"

"I already told him you two were no longer engaged."

Cora felt like she was having a mini stroke. She rubbed against the spot on her forehead that had started to pulse. "He was here?"

"Last night after you fell asleep. He wanted to wake you and I wouldn't let him."

"Why not? Don't you think he'd want to see me?"

"If he wanted to see you he would have been waiting at our office for your arrival. Instead, he was too busy working. When he did show up, he didn't seem concerned with your welfare, or the fact that waking you after what you'd been through was cruel."

"Hah, you expected Charles Dillard III to think about someone else's feelings?"

"Even more reason for him to take a walk."

"And he just went?" she scoffed.

"No, it took a little convincing, but not much. I explained to him that you were already planning on leaving him when you were kidnapped. It just delayed the inevitable. I explained that you would need to talk to him when you recovered, but that it would be a supervised conversation."

"I'm sorry, but he just accepted this?"

"No, not really. King and I made sure he understood that we weren't joking."

"And how did you do that?"

Van flashed his yellow eyes at her and his fangs dropped into his mouth. "Easy. Your ex doesn't seem to like Kindred very much."

"Aside from him being a speciest, Chaz doesn't just walk away from an investment. That's what he considers me. We already have some of the wedding planned. Hell, there are deposits that he definitely won't want to lose."

"I explained to him that you were mine now and there was no use for him to fight it."

Cora felt her brain take a long blink before she shoved her hand against his chest. It didn't get her much space because he seemed determined not to let her out of his arms.

"You told him. Like said the words?" Cora could feel herself starting to hyperventilate.

"I told him you were my mate and there was no use arguing."

"You...told...him...I wa-was your mate?!" The last word was rather high-pitched and a little hysterical.

"You *are* my mate, Cora. He was going to have to find out sooner or later."

Cora felt her heart starting to pound heavily in

her chest. Whatever reaction Chaz might have had in front of Van was not his real emotions. He wouldn't just let this go. Someone was stealing something of value out from under him. Chaz was ruthless when it came to things that he perceived to be his. But she had never seen him react to someone trying to steal her. It wasn't like she'd ever given him any reason to worry. Cora didn't flirt, she was always courteous, and for all the worries he might have had, she wasn't one of them. Until now. She knew what he would do if someone tried to steal business from him and Cora wondered if he would put up that much of a fight for her.

"Cora, you need to calm down. I have this all under control."

She didn't feel like calming down. She felt like screaming. So she did. Right in his face. "You can't just come in here and screw everything up!" she shouted. She could feel her eyes welling with furious tears and she didn't even care if Van saw her cry. She was mad and confused. What else was she supposed to do in this situation?

"Slow your breathing down or I'll do it for you," Van said seriously.

What was he saying? It was like he thought he was in charge or something.

"You can't just tell me to slow down my breath-ing. I don't want to slow it down! *I'm upset.* My life was already a fucking mess and you just threw my fucked up life in the blender and now I can't even recognize it!"

She was truly hyperventilating now, the air she was sucking in wasn't enough to fill her lungs so she was gasping for more.

Cora suddenly found herself on her back with Van's mouth over hers. She was already gasping for air, which gave him free access to sweep his tongue into her mouth. It also didn't let her gasp again. He kissed her hard for a moment before breaking free to let her take in air. She did, a huge lungful and then he was back at her mouth kissing her with a fierceness that had her toes curling and her pussy clenching.

She didn't even notice that her hands had slid into his hair, pulling him closer to her. It took a second for her to realize that she was kissing him back. Practically attacking him. Cora had forgotten what it was like to kiss someone you didn't know. Someone you hadn't been intimate with. It was the first time you were tasting, touching, and experiencing each other. It was good.

No, not good, it was fucking fantastic. Her body lit up at the pleasure that was coursing through her. Van would pause just enough for her to breathe and she would, but now her breaths were even and her heart no longer racing in a panic, but pounding hard inside her chest for a different reason.

"Van, stop," she heard herself say. Who the hell was this bitch telling him to stop? Her brain and her mouth were clearly not communicating.

"Why?" he asked, moving his mouth to her neck kissing over the spot she could feel was bruised.

"Because we aren't... together," she sputtered. She was saying the words while she was leaning away so he had better access. She was apparently trying to win the award for mixed signals.

"Hmm, aren't we?"

"Seriously, Van, this is too fast." Again, she was saying this was she was pulling at his hair. But not away from her, closer to her.

"I know you can't yet. You've been through a lot. I'm just trying to bring you a little pleasure. You know, endorphins can be effective painkillers."

What? Now he was trying to get to her with science?

"I still need to break up with Chaz," she said weakly. She really didn't give a flying fuck about Chaz. He was already becoming a past tense in her head.

"I broke up with him for you. The deal is done. We'll work out the details later. You're mine, Cora. I don't fucking share," he growled.

When he made that noise it made her want to squeeze her legs together. Anything to put pressure against her clit. It was like that rumble was linked straight between her legs.

"And do me a favor. Stop saying his name. It makes me want to rage. He's your ex and that is all we need to call him."

Cora didn't mind that. His name was stupid as hell and she felt like an idiot saying it. Four years of feeling like an idiot was way too long for anybody.

"I still don't think we should be doing this."

"You want me to stop, sweets, just say the word." He said this as his hand reached under the shirt and sweatshirt she was still wearing and cupped her bare breast.

Cora gasped. "Oh, sweet hell," she moaned. Van ran his thumb over her nipple as he squeezed.

"These are fantastic tits," he said kissing her lips.

"Just wait until you see them," she quipped, and then blushed. Shit, she wasn't supposed to be encouraging this behavior. This naughty, delicious behavior.

"Don't mind if I do," he said. Van unzipped her hoodie and lifted both her shirt and the sweatshirt over her head in a flash.

Cora was about to cover her breasts when Van captured her hands above her head.

"Don't you fucking dare cover those," he ordered.

The fact that she had such pale skin made the blush that was spreading from her cheeks down to her chest that much more apparent.

"Sweet and rosy," he said more to himself.

"Van, I'm not saying yes to... everything. I'm just..." she trailed off. She was being greedy as hell but she really didn't want to stop. She wanted to feel good. She wanted those precious moments when her mind would turn off and her body would turn on. It would be a vacation from her reality that she could really use right about now.

"I'm just giving you pleasure and you're accepting it. Leave it at that," he said, kissing her mouth in a way that wasn't soft or gentle. It was like he was sealing a deal.

Cora decided that this moment, that accepting Van and everything he had to offer was going to be the start of her new life. If he had really told her ex that they were through and that Van was claiming her, there was really no turning back.

When Van lowered his head to her breast she let go of the tension and fear she had been holding. She knew it would come back, but for that moment, she had control.

His mouth sealed over her nipple and that first

blank moment skipped over her mind. Instead of worry and doubt, there was only pleasure.

Van's mouth was working her as his hand cupped her ample breast molding it as he suckled. He alternated between her breasts and she squirmed to get loose.

"You going to behave?"

"I'm sorry, what?"

"Behave. Hands up, let me have these."

"Oh, that. Yeah, knock yourself out."

Van grinned at her and did just that. She laid back and just enjoyed it. The stiffness in her shoulders actually felt a little better with the stretch. She relaxed her arms over her head and left herself open to his hands and his mouth.

Both were doing some amazing things to her.

Van moved his way down her body and she let herself float away. His hand slid over her stomach, tickling over the smooth skin there. Then his hand dipped below her waistband.

Cora's hands itched to stop him. Not that she didn't want that contact. Her clit was aching to be touched and Van seemed willing and eager.

She felt his hand connect with the soft wetness between her legs.

"There she is," he growled into her breast.

"Van," she said sucking in a breath.

"That's right, say my name. Say the name of your man."

Cora wasn't sure about the 'your man' part, but she wasn't going to discourage him. "Van, that feels so good."

"Do you want me to make you come? I want to hear your heart stop the minute you explode. I want to feel your pussy squeeze my fingers so I can imagine my cock buried inside that honeypot."

"Did a bear just call my vagina a honeypot?" Cora giggled.

"No, sweets, your man just called it that. And it's mine now," he said sweeping a finger through her honey and bringing his hand to his mouth. He sucked on his finger and growled deep and low in his chest.

His eyes were closed then opened revealing his animal. "Better than honey," he said.

"I'll take your word for it."

"You've never tasted yourself?"

"Have you?"

Van paused like he was thinking. She almost laughed at that. "Can't say that I have."

"Well then..."

"It's different, believe me." Van leaned down and sealed his mouth over hers. She instinctively lashed her tongue against his getting a taste of what he was talking about.

Pulling back he nipped at the curve of her jaw, "My honey."

Van's hand went back into her pants and this time he didn't hesitate. His finger delved past her folds and sank into her tight hole.

"Oh, yes!" she cried, throwing her head back. Van pulled his finger back and added another, setting up a deep slow thrust. He pressed his palm against her clit and rubbed against it as he plunged his fingers inside her.

Cora would have thought it would take a while for her to build up any kind of response. She wasn't wired that way, but with Van there was no waiting. Her orgasm was heading towards her like a freight train. There was no stopping it and she was barely prepared when it hit.

She screamed, and screamed again until her voice cracked. It was harsh and possibly unattractive but she couldn't help herself. Her body was bucking and Van had faltered in his slow rhythm that was dragging her orgasm out longer than she'd ever experienced. To her knowledge she'd never come with such a slow calculated build.

"My girl comes hard," Van said, kissing over her face as she continued to jerk under him.

"I wanna see that every day. Multiple times a day. I'm going to make you come with my mouth. I want you to sit on my face and ride me until you explode. We'll fuck in every position we can think of then make up some new ones. Every damn day."

Cora was panting and her legs were still twitching. Van had pulled his fingers out of her but he was still cupping her pussy. "I think you are very optimistic about people's schedules, Van of Clan Rekkr."

"I'll make it happen, see if I don't."

Cora wasn't sure he would be able to pull it off. Then again, he was Kindred. There was no telling what he could do.

CHAPTER 14

Van was fucking proud of himself. He'd managed to not sink his cock into his woman. And she really was his woman now. He was hers just as she was his. But she was still recovering and he wouldn't do anything to impede that recovery.

Tucking her back into the bed, he kissed her forehead and whispered, "Sleep."

She smiled happily at him and drifted back off to sleep in no time. He knew it was greedy waking her, but he'd managed to doze off in the early morning hours, but his military training had made him a light sleeper, and he woke every few hours completely aware of his surroundings. Those surroundings happened to be a beautiful soft redhead snuggled up against him.

He knew there was no way in hell he was going to be able to get out of that bed and just walk away from her.

Once he had tucked her back in with that little smile still on her face, he went into her bathroom and took a quick shower. He wasn't about to let her sweet scent linger on him for any of his teammates to enjoy. Not until she was fully his.

Getting dressed, he knew he was going to need to get some clothes. He couldn't ask anyone to fetch and carry for him, so he'd have to do it himself. Walking quietly out of the room, he closed the door behind him this time.

He sent a few texts, and then rummaged around in the kitchen to find the supplies he needed to make a pot of coffee. He took note of the brand, the type of creamer she liked, and the bottle of liquid stevia she kept by the pot.

All the things that his mate liked were exactly what he needed to get for his place. Her sheets were nice, he'd have to upgrade his. He wanted her to feel at home in his bed, and in his kitchen, and in his arms.

Van had also started cataloging what was in her bathroom. At least the basics to get her started if she stayed over.

His phone rang after he took the first sip of his coffee.

"Talk to me," he answered after seeing it was King.

"So your mate's ex has been a busy beaver. We received a call from his father's lawyer stating they wanted a refund for what they had paid for Cora's retrieval."

"The fuck they did. What did you say?"

"I hung up. I don't have time for jokes in the morning. Then I got a call back from one of my sources. It sounds like Chaz likes to gamble. And when he ran out of his money, he started borrowing it to keep his father from knowing about his problem. One guess who he borrowed the money from."

"What a fucking idiot. Who borrows money from the mob? I mean, really? Take out a personal loan, max out your credit cards, but don't take money from people who take their interest percentage in broken kneecaps and body bags."

"They were obviously the ones behind the kidnapping, but I doubt they'll be willing to try for Cora again considering it didn't get them anywhere the first time. They'll move onto a new target," King declared.

"Agreed. I still want her watched. I have her covered most of the time. I'm going to try today to get her to stay at my loft. I won't need backup there and my place can be locked down easily enough."

"We're short staffed right now. I have Eden out on that pop singer gig. She's pissed as hell at me and calls regularly to curse me out. I had to remind her again that watching that bratty singer and drinking champagne really isn't that hard."

Van didn't want to disagree. He tried hard to stay off Eden's bad side. She was mean and vicious and could also kill you with her pinkie. Well, maybe not her pinkie, but certainly with one hand tied behind her back.

"What about Zion or Hudson?" Van asked.

"Zion called in, he thinks he'll be another week. He's got a lead on that missionary kidnapping. And Hudson has Baron up at the ranch training new recruits."

"Is Hudson training them or Baron?" Van asked because Baron was a German Shepherd that was sometimes more reliable than Hudson.

"I'm not sure really. They're due back in a few weeks."

"We should be good for now. I know we have work to do. I suppose I can stash her at the office if something comes up that you need me for."

"Stash her? You think you might want to run that by her first?" King suggested.

"She'll see I'm right about it. She's got to learn to trust that I know what's best for her." Van said this like it was obvious.

"Fuck man, this is going to get ugly," King sighed. "Why?"

"Because you can't seem to wrap your head around the fact that she isn't Kindred. Unless she's a groupie, she's probably never thought about being mated to one of us. Up until a few days ago, she had plans to marry her idiot boyfriend. You might want to back down on the telling her what to do if you don't want her to scratch your eyes out."

"I got this," Van assured him. He'd given her a great orgasm this morning. He should be good for a while.

"Damn, I should put money on this. I'll be in touch," King said before he hung up.

Van didn't have any doubts. How hard was it going to be to convince her that she needed to move in with him?

The doorbell rang and Van found the building manager standing there when he opened the door.

"Is Ms. Butler home?"

"She's sleeping, can I help you?"

"Can you make sure she gets this? It's important," he said handing over a large envelope.

"What is it?"

"It's for Ms. Butler, please," the man said. He didn't look comfortable being there at all.

Van nodded and shut the door. Tossing the envelope on the counter, he went back into the kitchen.

"Van?"

He looked up to see Cora coming out of the bedroom. She was wearing an oversized white t-shirt with a picture of an abstract Mickey Mouse over a pair of black cotton basketball shorts. Her stunning red hair was piled into a messy bun on top of her head. Looking at her, there wasn't a single thing he would have changed about her in that moment.

The fact she looked so adorable, so fuckable, and so completely at ease assuming he was still there, that was what was the most attractive. She was searching for him.

"Right here, sweets," he said walking towards her. He watched her cross her arms over her chest as her eyes darted up to his nervously. He didn't want that between them so when he got to her he pulled her into his arms.

Her head fit right next to his heart. She hesitated for a moment before she let her head fall against his chest.

"How did you sleep?" he asked.

"Which time?" she asked into his shirt.

Van smiled like the cocky bastard he was. "Either time."

"I feel better. I still feel like I could sleep for a month. But I had a bad dream and woke up. Then I realized it wasn't so much a dream as it was a preview of my immediate future."

"Something I can help with?"

"No, something I have to do. I have to talk to... him. I have to see him face to face."

Van thought that was a terrible idea. But he could see that if she was able to cut that connection it was only going to help his cause.

"I'll arrange something. Do you want do it today?"

"The sooner the better. I don't know what I'm going to do after that. I need to figure out a job, a place to live..." she trailed off.

"Let's start with breakfast. What can I make for you?"

She gave a little shove and looked up to him. "You cook?"

"I'm thirty-seven years old. I've learned how to feed myself. Nothing gourmet, but I can get the job done."

"I'll take anything, cereal, toast, just as long as it comes with coffee."

"Have a seat on the couch, I'll bring you a cup,"

he said. He tipped her chin a little higher with his finger and placed a kiss on her mouth. She didn't pull away, but he didn't expect her to either.

"Okay," she said. When he let her go, she went over and sat in the corner of the couch. She seemed to like that spot so he took note.

He made her a cup of coffee and grabbed the envelope as he went over to her. Handing her the cup she said a quiet thank you. He watched her take the first sip and sigh. "How do you know how I take it?"

"Kindred secret," he said. "This came for you while you were sleeping."

She set down the cup and took the envelope. "Who's it from?"

"The building manager dropped it off."

Cora tore open the top of it and pulled out a few sheets of paper. She started reading it then he saw her shoulders start to shake. He thought she was going to cry before she threw back her head and started laughing. Van felt a shudder roll over him. That laugh was still as beautiful as the first time he heard it. Not the same as that first moment, but it still hit him in his heart. His heart and then his cock.

"He's kicking me out," she wheezed.

"What?"

"It's a notice of eviction. *His* name is on the lease,

not mine. He wants me out in seventy-two hours or he'll get the authorities involved." Van watched her tilt over on the couch holding her stomach.

She looked crazy, the laughter was not matching the tears in her eyes.

"Cora?"

"What a prick!" she shouted.

"Yeah, we knew that. Cora, we found out that he's been gambling, and he owes money to some very unsavory people. People who thought that snatching you would get them the money he owed."

Cora looked at him in shock. "Fucking prick! Gawd, how could I have been so stupid. I'm not really surprised. He's always so cocky. He always said that he didn't lose. Losing was for quitters." She paused, shaking her head incredulously. "But really, three days?" She sat up and looked at him. "He wants me to find a new place to live in three fucking days?"

"You don't need to find a place. I have a place. It's big enough for both of us, at least for right now. I'll arrange to have your things moved over today. What doesn't fit, we'll store."

"Just like that?" Cora flopped back down on the couch and stared at the ceiling.

"Sweets, you were going to end up there anyway. This just moves things along."

"No, Van, I wasn't. I'm an adult. I make my own decisions. I'd rather move into a motel and look for a job then be beholden to you."

Van came over to the couch and leaned over her, giving her very little space. "Beholden?"

"Yes, like I owed you something. Van, I don't even have a job! I'll be lucky to get a minimum wage job. In fact, a motel might be out of my budget. Do people still stay at the YMCA?"

"That's it. You think you're funny, but you're not. I'm making breakfast. You pack enough for a few days and I'll get a moving company over here. I'm assuming everything in here is yours?"

"Nope. He technically owns all of this stuff. I don't know what he thinks is his and what is mine. I've had a credit card paid by him for so long I can't remember what it was like to count my pennies."

Van looked around the space. It wasn't fancy. There was no expensive art, or anything that looked overpriced. It was all very practical and looked reasonable for anyone that could be living and working on their own.

"Then you take your personal items. Anything you can't live without. We'll meet with him this afternoon and firm up the details. If there is something you need, I'll get it for you."

Cora made a groaning noise. "Don't you see? You

want me to go from being kept by one man to being kept by another! I won't trade one cage for another. That gives me zero control. I'm back accepting a situation to keep a roof over my head. Doing what you want when you want. No money of my own, no life of my own."

Van could see what she meant. "So you move in with me then get a job. I'm not some Neanderthal. You want to work, find something you enjoy. Take the time to not have to take the first thing that comes along. If you aren't sure what you want, I'm sure the clan can help you out. Once you're claimed and I make it official, they'll be your clan too."

Cora looked up him. "Claimed? What are you going to do, bite me?"

"Only if you want me to. No, claimed means that when I take you the first time and I come in you with nothing between us, you can't be any other Kindred's mate. Your mate mark will manifest to match mine. You'll smell like me, you'll be immune to some illnesses. After just having a little of my DNA inside you, you'll live over one hundred years. Our children will be like me. Then I'll announce my claim to the clan. They'll welcome you with open arms. If you want a wedding ceremony, we can do that too. It's up to you."

"Magical sperm?" She said with a giggle.

He smiled just a little at her laughter. "If you like. But you see why we don't let that out. You don't have to be a mate to get the benefits from a Kindred. If we do have sex with humans we aren't mated to, we only use Kindred made condoms. Extra strong and puncture proof."

"What kind of immunities?"

"I doubt you'll ever get another cold. If you're injured, my saliva or blood could temporarily heal you. We don't let that information out. It would put our people at risk."

She watched him, taking in what he was saying. Suddenly she reached up to her lip. The cut was gone.

"My cut! You did that?"

"Sometimes all it takes is a kiss to make things better."

"Dang, you should bottle that stuff."

"Again, that's why we don't let that secret out. It's for us and our families only. We can't have someone trying to snatch cubs to raise as their own personal first aid kits."

"No, I get that. It could be terrible. But, Van, I don't even understand what *I* want right now. I'm nothing short of a hot mess right now. Do you really want to take this on? I don't know if I would."

Van cupped her cheek. She looked so fragile

lying there. So unsure of what she should do. It wasn't fair what she had been through and it wasn't fair what she was still going through. Her life was changing moment to moment and he couldn't believe how well she was holding it together.

"Then take the time you need. We'll figure it out."

"You sound so certain," she sighed.

"I'm lucky that I can be. I know exactly what I want. I'm looking at her right now. My mind won't change, my heart won't change."

She looked like she was struggling to find the words to answer him. He didn't need anything from her, and he didn't need any assurances. That's how certain he was about the outcome.

"Don't answer. There's no need. Rest until I get your breakfast. Then you can take a nap while I make some calls."

She gave him a little nod.

"Good."

"Van? What's your mark?"

Pulling his shirt over his head, he showed her his chest. The design was iridescent, an infinity symbol in the center surrounded by interconnecting lines that reminded her of a Celtic knot.

"That's a nice one," she whispered. "I always loved how mates were proud of their marks. Wearing clothing that allowed the glimmer to show through. I always thought it was nice, nicer than flashing a diamond ring. Everyone knew it was permanent."

"It is permanent. A promise like no other. It's a promise we'll make to each other."

Van kissed her hard then stared into those blue eyes until she smiled just a little. He'd get her there, she'd trust him soon enough, and he was willing to be patient. "I'll make breakfast."

CHAPTER 15

C ora stared up at the ceiling, realizing that she was going to miss something as trivial as high ceilings. Van had basically just proposed to her. Could you do that to someone you met twenty-four hours ago? He told her secrets. He told her secrets *and* gave her an amazing orgasm. It hadn't been a bad morning. At least before the eviction letter. It didn't surprise her really. Chaz was cutting his losses. As far as he was concerned, a business deal that had no hopes of paying back its dividends should be expunged. His father would approve.

That's what was happening. She was being expunged.

She should feel bad about it. Any woman would be devastated at the loss of a relationship of four years. But if you haven't felt anything for six of those years, it really didn't count anymore, did it. Her heart just wasn't in it.

But then, where was her heart?

Maybe it was with the big man in the kitchen that looked like the type of guy you would avoid on the street because he could squash you with one hand.

He was kind to her. Gentle even. He was making her breakfast. Chaz had never made her breakfast. Sure, he'd ordered it a few times, but he'd never actually *cooked* for her. Or made her coffee.

She liked breakfast. She liked breakfast foods. Brunch was like a sport to her. She wondered if Van was a brunch kind of guy.

"Do you like brunch?"

"Sorry?" he called out.

"Brunch. Do you like it?"

"Eating breakfast late?"

"No, well yes. But I mean do you like to do brunch?"

"I never understood why people called it 'doing' brunch. But I like food. I don't really care when I eat it."

"I like brunch. I like brunch food. It's a mix of breakfast and lunch, hence the name," she started deciding to give him a mini lesson. "I like the really good ones that hotels have. The kind that have those waffle bars and omelet stations. Even better if there's a risotto station. I like the mix. The really good ones have seafood. That's when you know you're going to get your money's worth. Lobster, croissants, all the decadent things you never allow yourself to eat unless it's a special occasion. Start with breakfast foods, and then move right into lunch with mimosas on the side. Heaven."

Van came around the corner with two plates. He set one down on the table next to her. Two pieces of toast with butter and a thick layer of orange marmalade. Next to it were apple slices and peanut butter in a small dish along with some pieces of cheddar cheese. It was a weird collection of food, but at that moment, it looked like the best hotel banquet.

"I picked things that will give you energy. We can save the brunches for later."

"So you didn't answer me. Do you like brunch?"

"Sweets, if you like brunch, I like brunch. Eat."

Cora took a bite of toast. She chewed watching him as he wolfed down his food. He was watching her too, his eyes scanning over as though he was searching for something.

"If I say I like to take knitting classes, will you say you like them too?"

"Fuck no."

"What about if I say I want to go watch the ferries come in and eat caramel corn?"

"I'd say I'll arrange a time and make sure that the area is secure. We can go watch the stupid ferry boats. Although I don't understand the appeal of that."

"So... you'll like what I want to do if there is food involved?"

"No, I don't have to like it. I just have to like that *you* like it. You can take knitting on your own. You don't need me for that."

"Will you be waiting outside? Guarding my body?"

He made a low sound in his throat. "I'll always be guarding your body. It's mine."

"Rude, it's my body," she said biting her toast again.

"I now have a lifelong lease on it. We're joint owners."

"You're such a weirdo," she said.

"I know, but you seem to like it," he said.

She did. Van had given her more attention in two days than she'd gotten from Chaz in weeks. Maybe months.

"I'm confused," she admitted.

"You don't have to be. I've got you now. I'm your

man. It's simple. You want something I get it for you. You need something, I'll do it."

"And what do I do for you?" she asked. It was something she couldn't get out of her head. He was offering so much to a stranger. At least that was the way she saw it. Who was she? What did she have to offer?

"Stay."

"What?"

"You stay. You give me a chance. You don't think you have nothing to offer. Because you do. You have everything I need."

Cora shook her head at him. "I'm homeless, jobless, and I have zero prospects."

"Those things matter to humans. Not Kindred. I care about *who* you are, not what you can do for me. Since I've met you, I've seen a woman that was brave when she didn't have to be. A woman who screamed at men that had her under their control and didn't back down even when they took advantage of you and hurt you. I saw a woman who was willing to change her life because she didn't like the way it was going. And I also met a woman that was willing to accept help when it was offered."

He had her on that last one for sure. She was accepting his help because he was making it easy for her to do it. There were no hard and fast strings attached. Sure, he wanted the rest of her life as collateral, but at the moment, she didn't see that as a bad deal. Her life had been given a monetary value over the last week, and she wasn't sure she agreed with it.

Cora couldn't understand the big man sitting across from her. He had looks, muscles, a stable job, and a cool car. If you were a Kindred groupie he'd be a top contender. He could have any woman in the world if he set his mind to it.

The only problem, and granted it was a huge one, was that it was all happening too fast.

"Now, finish up and we can get packing, or you can take a nap. I'll make the calls to get a meeting set up."

"I can't sleep until this is done with. What if he doesn't come?"

"I'll threaten him."

Cora laughed. "Do you really think that will work?"

"I'm pretty sure he was about three seconds from pissing himself last night, so yeah, I think it will work."

"Damn, you're cocky."

"Sweets, you have no idea."

Cora smiled, and took another bite so she wouldn't say something that would end up with her back in the bedroom. Not that she hadn't enjoyed herself, because she had. Boy, had she. But it left her feeling instead of thinking, and right now, she needed to think.

There was the easy way; he was sitting across from her. And the hard way. The hard way wasn't a clear path. It was full of unknowns, and every scenario ended in the possibility of her begging for pocket change on the streets.

"Van?"

"Yeah, sweets?" he answered. He hadn't taken his eyes off her as she ate, she was sure of it. She kept glancing away because it was too intense. Too sexual. His eyes were eating her up.

"What am I going to do at your place?" She realized she was committing herself to going with him and she was pleased that he held back a broad smile before replying calmly.

"Whatever you want."

"I can watch TV? Do crossword puzzles?"

"Cora, you can do what you want. Within reason, of course."

"Within reason? What does that mean?"

"You aren't out of danger yet. Until I feel that your situation has changed, I want you with me."

Cora wanted to protest that restriction but she didn't want to hang out with bad guys against her will again, and honestly, she enjoyed Van's company.

"So, don't you have to work?"

"As needed. King understands."

"Understands what? That you are just going to take time off work for a woman?"

"Not just any woman; my mate. Kindred don't question the needs of mates. I need time? He gives it to me. I need coverage for you? He gives it to me. The same as I'd do anything he needed to help him protect his mate."

"He doesn't have one? That's kind of sad."

"I don't know about sad. Finding your mate isn't the same as human dating. Often it isn't something you can seek out."

"So, it's all random?"

"Not exactly. The Crones play a big part."

"Crones? What's that?"

"Who are they... They're the spiritual advisers of our clans. They commune with the creator and let us know Her will."

"Are they psychic?" Cora couldn't help but think that seemed to be an unfair advantage. Humans didn't get a telephone line to God to find suitable dates.

"I'm not exactly sure how it works. The Crones have been around as long as we have. When a Crone calls, it doesn't matter if you're a CEO or the head of your clan, you answer the call. Their word comes first."

"Wow, must be nice," she said.

"Nice?"

"To be heard."

Van set his plate aside and took her plate setting it with his. Kneeling before her, he pulled her close, wrapping her legs around his waist, her hands landing on his shoulders.

He was so close that she could barely breathe. Her center was pressed against his waist he was so tall. It took all her restraint to not rub herself against him like a cat in heat.

"Cora, I *hear* you. There won't be another man on the planet that will ever listen to you like I will. Your words matter to me."

Shit! She felt like she was going to cry. Van's words hit her harder than she could have expected. He hadn't said she was beautiful or sexy. He said that her words mattered.

"Van, what if my words aren't that important? I tend to rattle on, I know I do. I hate awkward silences. I always go off on tangents. Worse, I over-share about myself. In my mind I'm screaming for myself to stop but I never listen and it always gets awkward..."

"That's the kind of shit you need to get over. So what if you like to talk? So what if you want to share what you're thinking? No matter how small or mundane you think it is, I'm here to listen. Your words matter because *you* matter."

Cora felt a weight lift off her shoulders. She'd been told too many times over the years that she talked too much. That it wasn't proper and people didn't care about whatever tidbit she'd seen on the news or read on a website. Granted, she hadn't done her morning news dump on Van, but she got the feeling that he'd at least pretend to listen. That would be enough. She'd been so lonely that talking out loud had filled the gaps when she was in a room with a man who had made her feel so alone.

"Thank you."

"Don't thank me."

"I'm sorry," she stuttered.

"And don't apologize. There's nothing for you to be sorry for. You get to decide what happens right now. You tell me what's going to happen next."

Cora took a deep breath. He was giving her a choice.

She chose.

"Let me go pack."

CHAPTER 16

V an wanted to shake her when she said that she talked too much. A day ago he would have agreed that he didn't like anyone that talked about nothing. Idle chitchat wasn't efficient, and he hated wasting time.

But now? He wouldn't care if she wanted to read him the complete alphabetical listing of the Kindred Original Family lineage that every young Kindred was taught in school. Her voice was like a song to him. It soothed him and he would gut any man that told her she couldn't talk.

Kissing her gently, he pulled her to her feet and gave her a little shove towards her bedroom.

He took the dishes to the sink and rinsed them before putting them in the dishwasher. How long did she need to pack anyway? After what felt like an eternity of standing in the kitchen, waiting for her to come out, he gave into his curiosity and went into the bedroom to see what was taking so long. When he came in to her bedroom, he saw her standing next to her bed with her arms crossed. With an open suitcase and a few more bags at her feet. The bags were empty.

"Problem?"

"What do I take? I mean, what if I can't come back?"

"Sweets, you have seventy-two hours. Take the things that are most important to you right now, we'll get the rest later. Pretend you're just going away for the weekend," he said walking to her dresser. He pulled open the top drawer and start grabbing out the first things he saw. Items were tossed on to the bed.

"Van! Stay out of my underwear drawer!"

"Cora, really?"

She blushed and he kept at it. Grabbing bras and lacy things he wasn't quite sure about he emptied the drawer.

"Those are not the most important things. I just need some everyday stuff for now."

Van held up a strappy bodysuit and raised his eyebrows. "You're right, I'll buy you new stuff."

He opened the next drawer and started tossing things towards the bed again.

Cora rushed past him and shut the drawer. "Don't you have calls to make?"

"I'm helping you first. Then I'll take care of business."

"You're just messing stuff up. That's not helping."

"Sure it is. It's faster. You'll get this shit done so I don't have to help. Then we can leave."

"Is that the 'break a few dishes so you won't be asked to clean up' idea?"

"Basically. Don't forget bathroom shit. I don't have all your frou-frou stuff at my place."

"Frou-frou? You know that frou-frou is what guys like. They like us smelling like flowers and candy or haven't you ever seen a commercial?"

Van came over and got into her space. Sliding his hands around her neck, he used his thumbs to tilt her jaw up. He kissed her, hard and wet. Claiming her for a brief moment. When he was done he waited for her drowsy eyes to open.

"I like you smelling like you. I like how you smell when you're warm and aroused. Your pussy is the only honey I want. After that, I want you to smell like me. I want my scent all over you and inside you. My scent is your new perfume."

"That's kind of gross but it turns me on," she said her voice breathless.

"Good, this is your new reality, sweets."

He gave her ass a light slap and released her, heading for her closet.

"Seriously, Van. Don't mess up my closet! I have some very nice things in there. Don't take them off the hangers!"

Cora rushed past him into the walk-in and spread her arms wide, protecting her precious clothes.

"Baby, I'm trying to help you."

"I'll let 'baby' go this time. But it's not helpful when you're randomly throwing things! Give me a few minutes to get organized and I promise I will make some serious headway."

Van sighed. He liked touching her clothes; they smelled like her. But those clothes would be back at his house soon enough. He could be patient.

"Fine, I'll go see about arranging your meeting today. We can take what you pack in the SUV and I'll have Nadia find you a mover."

"Van, how am I...." she trailed off.

"You aren't. I'm paying for it because you're my responsibility. End of conversation."

He spun around and headed to the kitchen. The first thing after he'd claimed her was working on her money worries. Van didn't give a shit if she spent the rest of her life getting her nails done and waiting for him to get home. But he could already tell that kind of life wouldn't make her happy.

The dossier on her had all the charities that she was involved in. She liked working with kids, or at least she seemed to focus her attention and efforts there. There was no need for her to stop if it was something she really loved. He had more than enough money for both of them. King Security was one of the highest paid bodyguard companies in the country. They were often paid thousands of dollars an hour to keep people alive. Hell, sometimes it was even more just to babysit them so they didn't get themselves into trouble. The company covered most of his expenses which left his paychecks just sitting in the bank waiting to be spent.

It was about time he had someone he could spend that money on. Calling into the office he checked in with King about setting up the meeting. He reminded King that the meeting wasn't optional. He didn't want Cora worrying about the details after today.

"And if he says no?" King had asked.

"Remind him I'm happy to show up at his next business meeting and shift in whatever boardroom he's in. He doesn't want to say no to me."

King just laughed and hung up. Van got a feeling that fucker was enjoying this. Good for him, it was still too new and unsettled for Van's taste. He dialed the office again and got a very crisp Nadia working on finding Cora a mover.

"Cora? You done yet?" he called out. He wanted to go check, but he'd promised that he would give her space. He also wasn't sure that he'd be able to control himself around her. He wanted their first time together to be at his house. In his bed, in the place he paid for. It was going to be her space from now on too, and that's where he wanted to start their future. If he managed to get her pregnant, so much the better. That meant those memories would be started in Kindred space, and no one else's.

"I'm almost done!" She called out. She came bouncing out to the living room. Her eyes sparkled with something close to excitement, and she had a wide grin on her face. "I've got three suitcases. I want to grab a few boxes of my knickknacks. I'm sure I don't need to take them right now, but I don't want anything to happen to them."

"Then they go with us," he declared.

"I have some boxes in the spare room. Let me go grab them." She took off and he didn't bother to follow. He enjoyed the view too much.

She came back with a few boxes and stacks of old

tissue paper. "I guess it's good that I haven't taken my recycling out yet."

"What the hell is that from?"

"Gift bags. Every event I host or attend has a stupid gift bag. Expensive stuff for people that can afford to buy it themselves, but love getting a freebie. It's pathetic," she said shaking her head.

Van leaned on the kitchen counter and watched her moving around the living room pulling things off the bookshelves and the walls. She wrapped and stacked things in the boxes. A number of framed photos and photo albums went into the boxes.

She came back around into the kitchen and started opening and closing cupboards.

"Cora, what are you looking for? I have dishes at my place."

"I need my big cups. I have my hot cup and my cold cup. I also need my super big tea cup."

"These are all different cups? Can't you use just one?" he asked.

She turned to him and frowned. "Are you being serious?"

"I think I am. I mean I'm not saying don't take them. I'm just curious."

She started pulling down her cups. "See? Hot, cold, tea, and oh, I need my divider plate."

Van saw her looking back through the cupboards then searching the dishwasher.

"Found it!" She was holding a plastic plate with segmented sections like you would feed a child from.

He raised his eyebrow at her.

"What? Don't you ever get annoyed if your food touches? I mean not all the time, but sometimes it's important to keep it separate. It's like when you don't want to touch your food. I can eat pizza any old time, but some days I really don't want to touch it. Like my fingers getting greasy freaks me out."

"Good to know. I'll make sure we have lots of silverware in case you don't want to touch your food."

"Good. Okay, what else?" she said twirling around. She looked fucking adorable.

"Cora, come here." Van rested against the counter across from her, his arms and legs crossed. As she came towards him, he opened his arms and she slid in next to him like she'd done it a million times. Her arms wrapped around his waist and she tilted her head up to him.

"Damn, you're a beauty, sweets."

"I'm glad you think so," she replied.

"I know so."

"You don't think I'm weird?"

"What, because of some dishes? No, baby, I don't

think you're weird. If it makes you happy or keeps you sane then it's important. I'm glad you've agreed to come with me."

"I still might win an award for being the dumbest woman on the planet, but it doesn't feel wrong. I have to go with that right now since so much else of my life is upside down. I'm tired of overthinking everything, so I'm going with my gut."

Van cupped her face with one of his hands. "I hope it's a little more than your gut that is helping you make your decisions."

"Van... I..."

"I get it. Too soon. That's fine. But when you're thinking things through, just remember, *I'm* not unsure. I have no doubts and I'm fucking over the moon that I was the one that came for you yesterday. I was the one that got to hear that sweet laugh of yours and find what I've been looking for my entire life. Not for one second since that moment have I had an ounce of doubt. This is it. You and me, together."

"That helps, it really does, but right now I've decided that I'm just going to focus on today. I have enough on my plate that I don't need to start planning out my entire life all at once. If I survive today, I can think about tomorrow."

"That's fair. Let's get through today. I'll even

take you to lunch once we drop your stuff off and get settled. Anywhere you want."

"Anywhere?"

"Yeah, sweets, anywhere. As long as I can wear what I have on right now."

"Done." She gave him a squeeze and Van squeezed her back. One thing was for sure, this fiery redhead was going to keep him on his toes.

CHAPTER 17

Cora must have cracked while she was being held. Or maybe she died. Her go with the flow attitude was surprising even her. She was willingly going over to Van's house for an undetermined amount of time. Basically, she was moving in with him... and to top it all off, she was excited about it.

She wasn't so naïve that she thought this could be a temporary situation. Where the Kindred were concerned, nothing was temporary. Everything was permanent. It was one of the things she admired about them. Kindred didn't get divorced, they didn't backstab their own to get ahead. If there was someone that wasn't playing by their rules, they took care of it themselves. Back when the United States was creating the Declaration of Independence, there was another document that was drafted. The Kindred Freedom Act gave almost complete autonomy to the clans to govern themselves.

They still followed the rules of the land they inhabited, but there were instances where man's laws didn't apply. From the rumors that circulated, it was rare for anyone to break the rules laid down in the Act, and those punishments were harsh enough to keep everyone else in line.

Cora knew that moving in with Van was a statement. It was a commitment to him. She wasn't lying when she said she wasn't sure and she really hoped that over time her mind would catch up with how her heart was feeling, because there were warm fuzzies happening that she hadn't been prepared for. Van made her heart skip beats. She had to resist smiling like a crazy person when she saw him. She wanted to giggle every time she looked at him. It was bad.

She was going to have to get that shit under control.

On the practical side, being homeless was not something she was willing to face at the moment and taking Van up on his offer of employment wasn't completely crazy. Working with the Kindred would be like a dream come true. It was time she pulled her weight, and working for an actual wage was important to her. Though her heart broke a little at the thought of no longer being on the boards of the various charities she'd sat on while she'd been with Chaz. They had meant everything to her. Her only sense of self-worth the last few years had been knowing she made a difference. Not having that was going to leave a hole in her soul.

Her life with Chaz had made her lazy. The years had slipped by too easily without any growth. That had to stop now.

So, she was leaving it all behind to live with the hot bodyguard that had rescued her from a hellish situation. That seemed like something a desperate woman would do. And she had to admit, she was a desperate woman.

Van made her stay in the apartment as he hauled her boxes and suitcases down to the car. It wasn't until he'd checked in with Anson, who was still parked outside, that walked her out and she swore he'd somehow made his body twice as big as it normally was. As though he was her shifter shield. His SUV had also materialized in front of the building, the engine running at the curb.

She was deposited into the front seat and he was around the car sitting beside her in the blink of an eye.

"I don't like this location," he said as he pulled out into traffic.

"Well, I guess it's a good thing that I won't be living here anymore." It was a little sad. She'd been in that apartment for longer than she'd ever lived anywhere. Before that she'd spent two years living out of the city, claiming that she couldn't move closer because her lease wasn't up. That was almost true. She'd kept renewing the lease at her crappy little apartment an hour north of the city on purpose. It gave her a break from the Dillard world when she needed it.

Cora might miss the view, but she wouldn't miss the price tag that came with it.

"So where do you live?"

"Old SoDo, not far from the stadiums."

"Really? There are apartments down there?"

"There are warehouses. I bought one years ago. I turned half of it into a loft. The other half I rent out to companies that need to store things."

"Things?"

"Just freight, nothing illegal. Items the owners don't want in commercial facilities. It pays well and I have state of the art surveillance that a lot of my customers rely on. That's why I know that the most important thing in the world to me will be safe there."

Cora didn't assume that *she* was that 'most important thing,' but it was certainly implied. They drove through town and into SoDo, passing the baseball and football stadiums. Huge electronic billboards flashed, showing the human matches and the Kindred games coming up. Cartoonish beasts running down the field shredding the competition played for the Kindred game. They had split the leagues almost sixty years ago when humans kept getting hurt. Cora loved watching the Kindred Olympics. At least the opening ceremonies kept her attention.

"Do you watch the Seattle Sentinels?" Van asked.

"Occasionally. I like Kindred football, although sometimes it's a little too violent for my taste. Those guys really should wear helmets like the humans."

Van gave her a feral grin, "That would take the fun out of it."

Shaking her head, Cora looked out the window, and didn't see much in the way of amenities in the area.

"I'm going to have to learn the light-rail routes," she said looking out the window.

"I have cars. You'll use those."

"Well, maybe until I can get one of my own." She wasn't sure when that would be, so borrowing a car would be a better option than learning new bus lines. Especially since she wasn't sure the buses even came out this way.

"If you want something other than what I have, I'll get it for you."

"You'll buy me a new car?" she laughed at him.

"Yeah."

"Just 'yeah'?"

"Cora, if you need a car, I'll get you one."

"So, say I want a Lamborghini?"

"No. There's nowhere to park it and it's not safe. I'd prefer you have something that could withstand a collision. Have you seen how people in this city drive?"

Cora didn't comment that he had been whipping in and out of traffic at top speed the entire time they'd been in the vehicle. She had to assume it was something to do with his enhanced animal reflexes. That or he was just a lead foot.

They eventually turned into a small lot next to a large green building. It had a number of oversized garage doors. Nothing about the building would make you think it was anything but a storage facility. No signs, no obvious extra security beyond the razor wire topped chain link fence, but all the buildings in the area had that charming feature.

Van hit a button on his dashboard and one of the

smaller doors opened. He pulled in and the door closed behind them. A light automatically came on and Cora looked around the huge space. There were large metal shipping containers, racks with pallets of shrink wrapped boxes, and cars. Four of them.

There was a black two-door coupe that looked to be as fast as it was sexy parked alongside a truck with extra large tires. The gleaming red color of the truck's panels made it look intimidating. There was a slick silver four-door Mercedes and an oddly beige looking car sitting like an ugly duckling next to the rest... odd car out.

"You own five cars?" she said surprised.

"Yeah, I had to sell two. I never drove them."

"Huh, makes sense," she said sarcastically. "So, what's with that one," she asked, pointing to the ugly duckling.

"Close your eyes."

"What?"

"Go ahead," he encouraged.

Cora did, even though she felt silly.

"What color was that car?"

"I don't know, brown? No, light brown? It was ugly, I know that much."

"How many doors?"

"Two, well, maybe? They blended in."

"What did the driver look like?"

"Driver? It's empty but the windows were too dark."

"Exactly. It's ugly enough to not get noticed. That comes in handy. King may like his big SUVs, but even those stand out in some parts of town."

Cora opened her eyes to examine the car. She'd been pretty much wrong about everything. It was a four-door, and the color was much lighter than she imagined.

"Let's get you settled."

Cora gave a sigh. "I should probably change," she moaned. She'd thrown on a pair of yoga pants and a long sweater while she was packing.

Cora might have felt self-conscious, but with the way Van was looking at her, she was starting to think she could wear a sack and he'd would be happy. It was such a funny feeling. It was an absolute acceptance of who she was that she hadn't felt before. It was almost addictive. Her doubt monster was having a hard time getting a word in edgewise. She knew everyone had that doubt monster; it was just that sometimes she felt hers had a bullhorn.

"What's wrong with what you're wearing?"

"It's not something to be seen in," she explained.

"Who the hell is going to see you? The President? She's been known to dress down occasionally too."

"No, there is a certain way I'm expected to dress. Appearances matter."

"To who? Fuck that. Wear whatever the hell you want. Your choices now, remember?"

Cora hadn't remembered. She'd forgotten. Again. This was all so new to her, and it was going to take some getting used to.

"Interesting concept. I'll have to ponder that."

"Yeah, baby, you ponder that."

Van had a way of saying things that made her feeling goofy, and at the same time he wasn't being condescending. He should totally teach classes in this kind of behavior.

They got out and Cora started to grab some of her stuff.

"Baby, leave it. I'll get it. Let me show you around first."

Cora took her hand off her luggage and shrugged. She was so used to taking care of herself that it was a hard habit to break.

She followed Van to a door that cut the large building in half. There was a glowing pad next to the heavy metal door and he pressed his thumb to it then entered a code.

"I'll set you up with your own code. You pick the numbers."

"Can it be o-o-o-o?"

"No."

Van held the door open for her, and Cora smirked as she walked past him. But as she stepped into the other room, her mouth dropped open in surprise. She wasn't sure what she was expecting, but it wasn't what she saw. It was an enormous room with one wall that had huge, solid pane windows that started about ten feet above the ground, giving the room complete privacy, but tons of natural light.

A giant television took up one wall. There were two dark brown suede couches angled towards the TV. There was no coffee table; instead, the space between the couches was taken up by what looked like the world's biggest futon mattress covered in giant pillows of varying sizes.

It was a sleepover party's dream.

Cora turned to him with surprise written all over her face.

Van rubbed the back of his neck sheepishly. "Yeah, uh, I like to lay on the floor. Sometimes I shift and sleep out here."

"No way," she breathed.

"It's comfortable," he explained.

"Totally, I get that. It's awesome."

Van smiled at her. "I'm glad you like it. Kitchen is there, there's a bathroom over there, and the laundry is behind it."

Cora took in the modern kitchen with a long island that stretched the length of the kitchen, facing the open room. It stuck into the room and she could see the door to another room behind it.

Coming into the main room was a set of metal stairs. Van pointed up, "Spare room, gym, and office."

Then he walked to just under the stairs. "Here's our room."

Cora knew that she should have given him shit for his presumption, but it was so nice for him to immediately include her in his life. It was refreshing and touching at the same time.

The room wasn't huge, but it was large enough to fit a low profile California king that was set up to be a miniature version of the living room set up. There was a fluffy white duvet with at least six pillows stacked on it. Along the outside wall were the same windows as the living area, although here, the windows were frosted to prevent any prying eyes from seeing anything they shouldn't.

That wasn't the thing that caught her eye, it was something else.

"You make your bed?"

Van looked at her like she shouldn't be surprised. "Military."

"Ahh, makes sense."

"The bathroom is through here," he said, pointing to an open door. There was another door that she had to assume was a closet. She hoped it was a big one.

Stepping past him, she walked into a bathroom that felt bigger than her old apartment.

"Wow," she said turning in a circle. It was tiled floor to ceiling in dark slate tiles and one wall was taken up with a long counter that held two sinks with ample space between them and counter to ceiling cabinets on either side. There was a separate room for the toilet and along the back wall a huge walk in shower. It was big enough for a number of people. Beside the shower was a tub that could double as a Jacuzzi.

"Do you take a lot of baths?" she asked looking at him quizzically. He'd taken up position in front of the door as he watched her move through the space.

"Never used it."

"Then why did you build it?"

"Because I knew that someday my mate might use it."

Cora looked at him in disbelief. "Seriously?"

He shrugged. "You don't like it, don't use it."

"I didn't say I didn't like it. I'm just surprised you planned for the future that way."

"If you think that's good, follow me," he said as

he turned on his heel and walked out of the room. Cora ran to catch up. He was standing at the door she had assumed was hiding a closet. He pulled the door open and stepped aside so she could take his place. When she was where he'd been standing, he reached in front of her and flipped on the light.

Cora gasped, "Oh-my-giddy-od."

Before her was the closet of her dreams. It was as big as the massive bathroom with an entire luxury closet system package in white wood and glass doors. Long and short racks, built-in shelves, drawers, shoe racks, and in the center there was a lighted island with a glass top. As she stepped towards it she saw the top was designed with drawers that could be pulled out, velvet covering the bottoms to display jewelry. Smaller drawers under that would be perfect for lingerie.

Cora turned back to Van. He was leaning against the doorframe, his arms crossed with a smile on his face. Next to him was a four-foot section that held what could only be his clothes. They were mostly black and there was a neat line of boots on the floor.

"What the hell, Van?"

"Like it?"

"This is... I don't have words. You're saying you built this for your mate?"

"No, I built it for you."

"Well, shit," she said, feeling her throat start to close. Shit, she was going to cry... over a closet.

"Baby, it's a closet."

"No, it's not," she said, her voice cracking. "It's beautiful. It's something you thought of before you even met the person it was intended for. That's amazing."

"If you like it that much, it must be fate. It was meant to be yours."

Cora leaned over and laid her tear-streaked face on the top of the island, giving the surface a big hug. "I think you're right. I totally deserve this!" she said with a laugh.

Van smiled in a way that curled her toes.

"You aren't making it easy, you know," she said, straightening from her furniture hug.

"Why shouldn't all of this be easy?" he asked with a shrug.

"Van, let's be real for a second. I don't know anything about you and here I am moving in and laying claim to things that belong to you."

"To us," he corrected.

"Whatever. But really, it's not what..." she trailed off?

"Humans do?" he finished.

"Well, yes," she agreed.

"Aren't you glad I'm not human?"

Damn, she definitely was. She was glad his world was so different from hers. It did make it easier. All she had to do was accept that he was head over heels in love with her.

She shouldn't have asked what she did next. But it popped out.

"Van, do you love me?"

Van straightened from his place at the door. His eyes went from silver to yellow and he was across the room with her in his arms in a flash. His mouth was over hers and his tongue was tangled with hers before he took a breath.

"Cora Butler, I will fill you in on my entire life if you want. I'll video chat my parents tonight if you want to meet them. You can meet my sister and my brother-in-law and I'll show you all the pictures I have of my crazy nephews. My life is an open book to you. I don't care if you haven't read it yet. You will. Those are details that don't factor into the fact that I *love* you. You are my heart and soul."

"Wow," she whispered.

"I need you to get this. You are my heart and fucking soul. I wouldn't be able to live without you."

"Thank you?" Cora figured that probably wasn't the best response, but she felt like it needed to be said.

"You're welcome. You don't ever have to doubt

me, baby. And don't start that bullshit that it's not my free will. When it comes to mates, Kindred aren't controlled by someone else. Our mates are meant for us. We just get a little help in figuring out who they are."

"Okay," Cora wasn't going admit that she'd had that thought. What if he was under some kind of spell? What if he could fight it and change his feelings? What if he just suddenly snapped out of it? Whatever 'it' was.

"Okay?"

"Yes, Van."

"Good," he said, kissing her nose. "We need to head to the office. We've got shit to take care of."

'Shit' was an apt word. Cora felt her stomach start to curdle.

"You need something to eat before we go?"

Cora shook her head. "No, don't think I could."

"Baby, I'm going to be right there. Nothing is going to happen to you and I wouldn't let him talk to you in any way I thought was disrespectful."

"My hero," she sighed.

"Always."

Cora wanted to spend more time in the closet. It was big enough that she could camp out in there if she wanted. Maybe that was something she'd have to talk Van into. Add a comfy chair and light so she could read in the cozy space if she wanted.

"Let's get this over with," she said.

"Are you going to change?" he asked, a smirk on his face. She could tell that he wasn't used to smiling because he always looked a little uneasy when he did it.

"Fuck no," she said firmly.

"Good girl, let's go."

CHAPTER 18

Van was happier than a pig in shit. Cora liked his place. He'd told her the truth. With every detail, aside from the living room, he'd thought of his possible future when designing and building.

If she had hated it, he would have torn it all down and started over. Or moved. Whatever she wanted, he would have done it. It didn't matter how much he liked his place. He could adapt to anything. She needed to be comfortable. Humans liked to say, "Happy wife, happy life." The Kindred had a saying too, "Happy mate, don't tempt fate." Meaning that there will never be a more perfect match for you, so it was in your best interest to keep that person happy.

Cora might be unsure about her part in everything, but it was his job to reassure her until she saw the truth.

As they drove back to the office, Van's current truth was that he didn't want her anywhere near her ex. It upset her and by extension, upset him.

He wanted it over and done with. He wanted the ties to her past severed once and for all, however that had to be, and then he could claim his mate.

Van pulled in and parked. Cora jumped out and Van met her on her side of the SUV. "Baby, don't get out of the car before me."

Cora looked up at him confused. "What?"

"Don't get out of the car first. Wait for me."

"Is that some sort of chivalry? 'Cause I like it."

"Call it what you want. But I get out first, I assess the situation, and then I decide if it's safe for you to get out."

"What, like every time?"

"Every time."

"Say we go to the grocery store, are you going to secure the parking lot before we shop for toilet paper?"

Van stared at her like this was not a hard concept. "Yeah, baby. Me, then you."

"So you're in danger before me?"

"Do you turn into a six hundred pound bear?"

Cora pretended to think. "Fine, you got me there."

"Good, now stop sassing me and get in the elevator."

He walked behind her while she grumbled under her breath about how much she was going to sass him.

It was fucking cute.

Inside the elevator, he inserted his keycard and hit the button.

"I want you to wait in King's office until I come to get you."

"Is that an order?"

"It's a request. I want to..."

"Assess the situation," she finished for him.

"Smartass."

"Better than a dumbass," she said with a grin.

Van couldn't wait for the rest of his life living with this kind of constant banter. He didn't mind talking to her. Everyone else could take a flying fuck at a rolling donut. If his mate liked to chat; she'd chat with him.

As they entered the lobby and Cora waved and smiled a hello to Nadia. Nadia gave her a small smile then looked at Van. Her eyes shot open and a look of fear and astonishment crossed over her face.

He stopped in his tracks. "What?" he barked at her.

"You... you're *smiling*," Nadia said like it was a dirty word.

Van realized she was right. He'd walked into the office with a grin plastered on his face like a crazy person.

"Isn't he handsome when he smiles?" Cora asked.

"Oh, uh, well..." Nadia trailed off. She looked like she was going to be sick.

Van knew that Nadia probably wouldn't answer something so personal so he saved her from it. "King in?"

"Y-yes, your one o'clock is in the conference room. King is with them."

Van nodded and took Cora by the elbow. He walked her down the hallway to King's office and sat her in one of the chairs across from his desk. Van leaned over her and tipped her chin up to look at him.

"We got this. You aren't alone. I'm with you. Me, and you. Fuck everyone else."

"Fuck everyone else," she repeated.

Van gave her a kiss that left her pink cheeked and panting. "Damn, you look good like that."

"Thanks," she said, her eyes still a little glassy.

"Baby, you gotta stop thanking me."

"Yeah, that's probably not going to happen."

Van shook his head and left the room, marveling at the creature that the Creator had picked out for him. Every word that came out of her mouth was pure poetry to his ears, but he knew that if it had come from anyone else, he would have hated them instantly.

Van walked to the conference room and stepped in without waiting. He wanted the element of surprise.

He found King sitting at the head of the conference table. Sitting at the opposite end, at the far end of the room, pale and sweating, was Charles Dillard III. Clearly there had been a power struggle. Van almost laughed.

"King," he said, addressing his boss first.

"Van," King said dryly. He looked annoyed, his jaw set in a clench that told Van that Mr. Chaz Dillard was already pissing him off.

Turning to the other man, he took in the two suits that were sitting side by side to the left of him. He'd brought lawyers, what a punk.

"Mr. Dillard."

"Where is she?" Chaz barked.

"Nice to see you again. You look well." Van was happy to annoy this little shit.

"Where. Is. She."

"I'm going to assume you mean Ms. Butler. She's here. I just wanted to set some ground rules before I bring her in. There will be no name calling, no nastiness, and if I see anything less than absolute respect being paid to my mate, I will end this meeting."

Van scanned over the lawyers and saw both of them swallow. Chaz must have left out the part about Cora being his mate. They looked surprised.

He could see Chaz grinding his teeth. "I have things to do."

"I bet you do. Busy little beaver, aren't you?" Van asked.

Chaz didn't answer. Smart. Van shot King a look before leaving the conference room. He found Luca standing across the hallway, his casual wall lean, anything but.

"Need something?" Van asked.

"I don't like that guy," Luca grunted.

"Join the club."

Van walked past him to King's office and opened the door carefully. Cora must be nervous and he didn't want to startle her.

"Baby, let's do this."

She nodded and stood. He took her hand and walked her past Luca. Van saw her give him a wave and Luca lifted his chin her direction. That was almost as good as a hug for Luca.

Van opened the door and walked Cora straight to the end of the table beside King. He sat her next to him and took the seat on her other side, putting his body between her and her ex.

Cora sat primly, her hands in her lap.

"Chaz," she said.

Her ex didn't bother to respond.

One of the lawyers cleared his throat, "Ms. Butler, Mr. Dillard would like to dispense of these proceedings as quickly as possible."

The lawyers looked the same to him, so Van didn't give a shit what their names were.

"I just need to know what I can take from the apartment and what the situation with the credit cards will be." Cora said. Her voice was strong, even though Van could hear the slightest tremor in her voice, one that no human would be able to pick up.

"I don't give a shit about the stuff in the apartment. Although, I did pay for all of it. She decorated it nicely enough, it might be a good place for me to take dates."

Van wanted to punch him in his smug little face.

"I realize that you paid for it, Chaz. I would never say that you didn't. But we did pick out a lot of those things together," Cora said.

"You didn't work!" Chaz spat.

"You didn't *want* me to! You said it would make you look bad. I still worked, I just worked for free. I was on the board of a dozen charities that your family is involved in. I worked the social side of your life, just like your mother does. You know that I did."

"Whatever," he shot back.

Lawyer number two coughed and started talking. "Ms. Butler, Mr. Dillard would like you to vacate the apartment, taking whatever belongings you want. He would like for you to pay the outstanding credit cards that are in your name, totaling twelve thousand, four hundred and eighteen dollars, along with the remainder on the wedding dress you destroyed, totaling ten thousand dollars."

"I didn't destroy that dress! You asshole. I was kidnapped! Because of you!" Cora screamed, her demeanor changing in a flash.

"That hasn't been proven," Chaz sneered. "Maybe you pissed somebody off, did you ever think of that?"

"I can't believe you!" Cora was halfway out of her chair when Van put his hand on her shoulder and gently pushed her back down into her seat.

"Baby, settle," he said with a laugh.

Cora's eyes blazed into him, "You think this is funny?"

"No, I don't think it's funny, I think it's pathetic. He's lashing out because he apparently doesn't understand," Van said to calm her.

"I don't understand what?" Chaz barked.

Van looked over at King, who took over the meeting.

"Mr. Dillard, I'm not sure if these lawyers know about your recreational activities, but to put it *very* simply, *you* were the cause of Ms. Butler's abduction. You're not in any financial situation to demand any money of Ms. Butler. That is, unless you'd like your activities shared with the public, including your father."

"You can't do that! Isn't there some kind of client confidentiality?" Chaz sputtered. The threat of having to tell his father about his failings was finally making him start to look a little nervous.

"You waived that privilege when you threatened not to pay us for services rendered," King said firmly.

"I believe the payment was made to your account, Mr... King," Lawyer number one stammered.

"It was. But your client hired us to do a job. That job is over." King wasn't going to play with these guys, and Van was happy to sit back and watch.

"It's not over if my fiancée isn't back home where she belongs."

Van looked over to Chaz. "You mean the home you just kicked her out of? Ms. Butler was safely retrieved. Once she was back at our office she made it clear that she didn't want to be picked up by Mr. Dillard. That is beyond our control."

"And you telling her that she was your mate wasn't some kind of plan to get back at me? She's probably not even your type!"

Van growled and King stepped in. "Van, don't."

King may have been Van's boss, but he didn't have control over his personal body. Though reminding him that they were there to resolve things, not make them worse, was important to note.

"Never, *ever*, doubt a Kindred's claim to their mate," Van growled, his bear vibrating through his voice.

"Whatever, I just want this done," Chaz said dramatically.

"Need I remind you, Mr. Dillard, that we could drag this out. As far as the State of Washington is concerned, you and Ms. Butler were in a Committed Intimate Relationship. It wouldn't be too hard to prove that you had provided for her the past number of years... Ms. Butler could be entitled to half of your assets. Don't make us get the legal system involved," King warned.

Lawyer number two spoke up this time. "We

don't feel that will be necessary. As we said, Mr. Dillard isn't asking for much considering he has willingly supported Ms. Butler for the last four years."

"Agreed," Van said. "Any credit cards in her name will be paid along with the remaining cost of the dress. She is allowed to take anything in the apartment that isn't nailed down. If she wants it."

Lawyer's one and two looked at Chaz who flicked his hand in the air. "Whatever, like I care. I was done with her anyway. She wasn't marriage material. My mother will be thrilled."

"Chaz, you are a Grade-A jackass. Good riddance," Cora said.

"Nice one, sweets," Van said proudly.

"Babe, if I'm a jackass... well, you're the one who stayed with me."

Van growled. "I see why you don't like being called 'babe.'"

"I know, right? Like nails on a chalkboard."

"Fine, then is there an agreement?" lawyer one asked.

Van looked to Cora who replied, "As long as I can get my stuff and the things I care about. After that I can happily not look back."

Those words were for him, and he knew it. It meant a lot. "Done," he said quietly to her.

"Wonderful, super! Let's wrap this up. I have

things to do," Chaz said. He was slouched in his chair now, as though everyone else was putting him out.

Van felt even sorrier for Cora that she had put up with this guy for so long. That was all over.

"We have a few documents to sign, then we can make copies for both parties," lawyer number one said.

Cora reached for Van's hand. Apparently she wasn't worried about upsetting her ex anymore, and that meant she was looking to him for comfort. He took her hand and gave it a squeeze.

The paperwork was signed and Chaz Dillard stormed out with his middle finger raised high.

"Classy guy," King said watching the two lawyers trail behind him.

"I don't trust him," Van said. Cora was tucked under his arm, and she was squeezing him tight.

"You shouldn't," Cora said quietly.

CHAPTER 19

Cora felt a little sick, but she also felt a little lighter. The paperwork was signed. It was probably easier than a divorce, which was what it felt like. She wasn't sad that it had ended. She was sad that it had taken her so long to decide to leave. The time she had given wasn't time she would look back on fondly, and that was the worst part.

Her future might not be certain, but it was open. Well, sort of open. The big man next to her seemed to think that their future was already decided.

Cora knew enough that if you were mated to a Kindred, you were beloved for the rest of your life. That didn't sound bad to her at all. *Beloved*, it was a word that was used freely when speaking about mates. She never saw a mate that didn't look at their partner with absolute devotion.

That wasn't something to turn your nose up at.

"Let's go see if Nadia has made any calls for movers," Van suggested.

They walked to the front of the office, which was empty except for a woman sitting on one of the couches. She was perched on the edge of the couch cushions, looking around nervously, her eyes darting to them as they entered. They lightened when Van walked in, and then narrowed when she saw Cora.

Cora didn't want to be unkind, but the woman had on way too much makeup, and her skirt was shockingly short. It barely covered her bits as she sat.

Looking over at the reception desk, Cora noticed that there was no Nadia keeping watch.

"Where did Nadia go?" she asked.

Van turned around to speak to the woman waiting on the couch.

"Did you see where the receptionist went?"

"She said she was going to get me some water, but then some hot Latino man strolled through and she went running. Haven't seen her since," the woman said. She tried batting her obviously false eyelashes at Van.

"She'll be in the recovery room. Cora, do you mind?" Van asked her.

Cora crossed over to the hallway and walked straight to the room she had just been in the day before.

She knocked softly and leaned in to hear if Nadia was in there.

"Yes?" came a quiet reply.

"It's Cora, uh, are you okay?"

"Yes... I think. I mean, is he still there?" Nadia asked.

"Who? Van? He's out front," she replied.

"No, not Van. Luca," she said the name like it belonged to the devil himself.

"Oh, I didn't see him. Just someone waiting in the lobby. A woman."

The door cracked open. "That's just a groupie," Nadia said. She stepped into the hallway. She was petite and only came up just past Cora's shoulder. She wore a high-necked dark blue blouse with a black pencil skirt that went just past her knees. The effect made her look even smaller. Her hair was pulled back in a bun, every bit the corporate professional.

"A groupie?"

"Someone that comes in with a story about needing a bodyguard thinking that one of the guys will end up as their mate."

"Don't they know that's not how it works?" Cora asked.

Nadia shrugged. "You'd think so, but they keep trying. They also think that if they can get a Kindred pregnancy that the men will stay with them. That's not how it works either."

"I've never heard of a non-mated baby."

Nadia gave her a small smile. "It doesn't happen anymore. Modern technology and all," she said quietly, imparting a secret that few probably knew.

"Ahh, so what's up with you and Luca?"

When she said the name Nadia shuddered just a little.

Cora was concerned at her reaction. "Is he mean to you? I can tell Van or King, they can do something about it."

"No, he's not mean. He just... scares me," she said in a whisper.

Cora could see that about the man. He was a big like Van. Someone as tiny as Nadia wouldn't stand a chance against him. Still it was a bit of an extreme reaction considering they all worked together.

"Has he hurt you?" Cora would happily sic Van on anyone that wasn't treating a woman right. She knew enough about him already that he'd never tolerate it.

"What? No, of course not. I mean King and the other guys would never allow that. They're always nice to me. It's just Luca, for some reason he freaks me out. He's quiet, always watching. He never misses anything. It's unnerving. I don't think he likes me. "

"I get that. Some people just rub you the wrong way," Cora offered softly.

"I'm sorry, you must think I'm silly. I just found that if I avoid him I feel better."

"I've been known to hide at parties from people that I don't want to talk to, so I understand completely."

"Thanks, you're nice. I'm sorry I wasn't there to greet you."

"Well, he's gone. And by the way, I don't need a grand reception when I come in. I'm sure we're going to be seeing a lot of each other from now on," Cora offered.

"Thanks," Nadia said, as she walked to the front. As soon as she was behind her desk, she was back to business.

"How can I help you?" She directed her question to Van.

"Movers?" Van asked.

"I called three reputable companies. This one said they could come today on short notice," she said pushing a piece of paper across the counter.

Van looked it over. "Good, call them and give them the address. Do you want to be there?" Van asked Cora.

"Honestly, no. But I'll go because I don't want to forget anything."

"Have them meet us at her place in two hours. I'll be there to let them in."

"I'll make the call now," Nadia said picking up the sleek phone and dismissing them.

"Let's get some lunch then head over," Van suggested.

King walked into reception and kept his eyes on the woman on the couch. "Mrs. Cook?"

The woman stood and tried to smooth her skirt down over her hips. "Miss Cook. You can call me Madeline," the woman practically purred.

King didn't call her Madeline, he simply gestured towards the hallway. "This way, we can meet in the conference room."

The woman slinked towards him trying to swing her hips while she balanced on her stiletto heels. She had the look of a newborn giraffe.

King followed the woman with a pointed look back to Van.

As soon as they were gone, Van leaned over the desk to Nadia. "Put me down for old high school stalker."

"Got it." Nadia said, clicking on her keyboard. "I'll post the grid in the locker room when everyone has weighed in. I'm going with former photographer that used to shoot her when she was a model," Nadia said.

"I'm sorry, what's happening here?"

"Groupie pool. What she's going to say to King about why she needs protection. They never follow through, our prices are... above average," Van explained. "We keep a board in our locker room with the ongoing pool. It's our own little stress reliever."

"You guys are shooting too high. I'll take heavy breather on the phone. She doesn't seem like the type to figure out the whole stalker scenario."

"I'm sorry, do you get to play now?" Van asked.

"Are mates not allowed?" she asked innocently.

Van growled at her and she knew it was because she had called herself a mate.

"We're leaving," he said, grabbing her hand.

"Bye, Nadia! Thank you for your help!" Cora managed to call out as she skipped along behind him.

Van pulled her into the elevator and as soon as the doors closed, he picked her up and pressed her against the wall. The elevator didn't move and Van reached over and hit a button beside them.

Cora didn't have a choice so she wrapped her

legs around his waist. Van kissed her then. It was hard, open mouthed.

She kissed him back because it felt so good. He liked kissing her, she could tell. She could feel the length of him against her core and for the first time could get an idea of how big he was.

He wasn't average for sure. She wiggled against him because her body wanted her to. Her pussy demanding more contact.

"Sweets, I'm not claiming you in the elevator."

Van moved his mouth to her neck and Cora whimpered.

"Why not?"

"Because it's a fucking elevator. My mate does not get fucked in an elevator."

"What if your mate needs you and demands it?"

Van made a rumbling noise; his eyes flashed gold at her. "After you're claimed I'll fuck you anywhere you want except in public. I'm not into that."

"Good, neither am I. I don't know what's wrong with me. I'm achy, and just being around you makes me think all sorts of naughty thoughts."

"That's because we're meant to be together. We're meant to be one. As soon as we get our business taken care of, I'll make sure you are mine."

"What if I need something before we get our shit done? Something I want?"

Van kissed her hard again. "I don't want to risk it, not here. Besides this elevator has cameras."

Cora almost ducked at his words. Shit, she didn't think about cameras. "Fine, get me into a big car with a good backseat, fast," she ordered.

Van hit a button beside them and the elevator started moving. He didn't let her down; he kissed her through the remaining floors until they hit the garage. His hands moved on her, his body blocking her into a corner. His kiss was one to taste her, drink in her essence.

"Is this elevator private?" Cora realized when they hit the bottom.

"Yes, I wouldn't have even kissed you if I thought it could open on another floor."

"That's so sweet, protecting my modesty," she teased.

"You're mine, I don't share. Especially when you don't have my mark on you yet."

Cora was starting to think that her mark was going to be inevitable. Especially if she couldn't keep her hands off him. It had started when he had woken her up. It was like she got a hit of him and the cravings hadn't stopped since.

She wanted to see what was under those pants. Cora could tell there was something very exciting under that zipper.

The doors to the garage opened and Van was dragging her along again, except this time she was laughing at his urgency.

Van picked a black SUV parked in the far corner against the wall. He opened the back door and picked up Cora and placed her inside.

"Van!" Cora laughed.

He followed her and shut the door behind him. It was just dark enough in the garage that those silver eyes were glowing in the dark at her.

"Those eyes are amazing," she breathed.

"Glad you like them," he said, his voice all predator. "So what does my woman want?"

"Lay back," she said.

"What?"

"Lay back, or are you worried that it's a submissive position?"

"The fuck are you going on about? You want to play submissive we can play, I'm just not sure what you want."

"I want to see you, taste you," she said.

Those silver eyes disappeared for a moment. He must have closed them. "Van?"

"Just a second, I need just a second."

Cora grinned into the dark. That had to be a good sign.

The eyes came back and he said, "Are you sure?"

"Of course I'm sure," Cora said, trying to make her voice sultry. She wasn't sure if she was pulling it off convincingly or not.

"You're too good to be true," he said, his voice heavy.

She was totally pulling it off.

Cora gave his chest a little shove and he leaned back against the car door. His one leg stretched along the length of the seat and the foot on the floor. Cora got comfortable on the seat facing him. She leaned over and put her hands on his thighs, running her hands up towards his waist confidently, making sure to move her hands over the bulge under the fabric.

It was more than a handful and she hoped she could do it justice.

Cora reached for the zipper of his pants. She flipped the button open and grabbed the tab and pulled.

Van was holding incredibly still under her, as though he were carved of stone. His arms were spread wide, one on the headrest of the driver's seat and the other hooked over the back seat.

Cora glanced up at him and gave a smile. She was pretty sure he could see it, even in the dark.

"Can I?" she asked.

"Sweets, that belongs to you. Do whatever you want."

Cora reached up to the waistband of his briefs and pulled. She kept going until his erection sprang free. She had been correct in her assessment. He was huge. His cock was long and thick. She ran her hand up the shaft, enjoying the silky heat of his member. Attempting to wrap her hand around him, she came up short.

"Wow."

"Baby, really?"

"Yeah, that is worth a wow."

Cora felt like she'd just been given an award. She felt like she should give a speech or something.

Instead, she leaned over and licked over the end of his head. She heard his sharp intake of breath, so she did it again, this time swirling her tongue around the tip. Adding her other hand she figured out how best to bring him pleasure. There was no way she was going to fit his entire length in her mouth. She was going to have to get creative.

Cora started at the base and ran her tongue up the underside of his shaft. Teasing just under his head until she felt his hips buck. Giving herself a small pep talk, she opened her mouth wide and took as much of him as she could. She used her tongue and her hands to touch as much of him as possible.

She had an ear open to hear if he was enjoying

her or not. All she could hear was the creak of the leather seats where his hands were grabbing them.

"Fuck, Cora, you're killing me. I can smell you, you're wet for me," he growled.

Pulling off, she took a deep breath. "Is it okay? Am I doing..."

She didn't get to finish because Van's hand came down to touch her face. "Babe, I'm trying not to flip you back on this seat and fuck your brains out. Everything you're doing is perfect."

"Wonderful, if you have any notes after, I'll be happy to review them."

Cora couldn't help teasing him. It seemed to be how they worked together best. She returned to the thick length of him and did her best to focus on bringing him pleasure and not the dampness between her own legs.

It would be taken care of soon if Van had anything to do with it and Cora was actually looking forward to it. Being in the same room with her ex had made it totally clear that she deserved more. The man she now had in a very intimate position was offering her so much more.

Just that thought alone made her want to make him happy. She knew without a doubt that she was always going to be getting more in this relationship than she'd be giving. It was just the way of the

Kindred. They had the ability to sense things and assess needs that humans just didn't have.

Cora didn't mind playing catch up as long as she could play.

"Damn, sweets, that is good."

Cora hummed deep in her throat and Van growled. She did it again, this time moving her hands in time with her mouth. She loved that he had started to move with her, as though he couldn't resist any longer. She wanted him to lose his control. Lose that ability to face everything so stoically.

She wanted to know that she had an effect on him.

"Sweets, you might want to stop," Van warned.

Cora wasn't going to stop. There was no way she wasn't going to show him that she wanted this as much as him.

She didn't even mind that he was moving, cautiously thrusting into her as his moans got louder.

"Cora..." Van warned again.

Cora didn't stop as she held tight and got the first taste of her man. She licked and swallowed, loving him the best she could until he was done.

She gently kissed the end of his cock and rested her forehead against his stomach. She felt his hand rest against the back of her head.

"Baby, anytime you want to play, you just let me know. I'll rearrange my schedule," Van said.

Cora giggled. "Good to know I don't have to book it with your secretary."

"I don't have a secretary."

"Perfect, direct bookings."

Cora felt him kiss the top of her head. "What can I do for you now?" he asked.

She leaned up to look at him. "Honestly? Get my stuff moved so we can go home."

"You sure?"

"Not really, but we have movers to meet."

CHAPTER 20

Three hours later, Van was still trying to control the urge to mount his mate. They had made it to Cora's place after she had literally rocked his world in the garage. He shouldn't have let her do that, certainly not there. But he knew that the cameras couldn't see inside the cars through the tinted windows.

She also seemed like she needed to prove something to him. As far as he was concerned, she didn't have to prove anything. She was already knitting her life to his. Every time she took a step forward with him he knew that it was part of their fated relationship.

They arrived at her apartment and she had started moving things around and arranging piles before the movers even showed up. When they arrived, they were an efficient team, creating boxes and packing anything she pointed at.

"I want the spare bedroom furniture, but not master. I want the living room furniture and then anything else that isn't attached to the walls. Don't forget the televisions."

"If we can't make it fit in my place, we'll move some of my stuff," Van told her.

"It might be good to have a little break from these things. At least until some of the memories fade."

Van could understand that. Kindred had long lives, and they rarely got attached to physical items. It was more important to value their feelings and their relationships than to worry about stuff.

"Good thing I have a warehouse," he said, hugging her tightly against his chest.

"Good thing you have a huge closet," she laughed.

They had finished up with the movers. Everything had been packed within a short amount of time with the efficient team and they were on their way to Van's place.

Once there, he directed the movers to unload everything in the garage bay so that Cora could pick and choose what she wanted to bring inside.

He tipped the movers and told them to have a

beer on him. They had worked late and made a potentially difficult task easier for his mate.

They had grabbed sandwiches before hitting the apartment so Van just had to figure out dinner for his mate.

She deserved candlelight, expensive wine, and a meal to make a memory out of. But the circles under her eyes as they drove back said she wasn't going to be up for it.

Once the movers were gone, he used the bathtub for the first time. He filled it with hot water and then helped his mate undress. It was the first time he got to see what was now his, and he wasn't disappointed.

She was curvy, her full breasts tipped with sweet pink nipples. Her waist dipped in but flared out to her generous hips and thick thighs. Between her legs was a short patch of red hair. He wanted nothing more than to bury his face there for the rest of the night. But, first things first.

He helped her into the tub and then turned down the lights, which he'd had installed on dimmers.

"Take your time," he said, and then left her in peace.

Van went around the loft, lighting candles and turning down lights. It was late enough that if she wasn't hungry, they could go straight to bed. He didn't mind the idea of holding her all night long. If she wasn't ready to be with him yet, he'd wait. It was that easy. No, fuck that, it wouldn't be easy. It would probably by the hardest thing he'd ever done in his life. But for her, he'd do it.

While she was in the bath, he changed the sheets on his bed to the nicest ones he had. He still needed to shop for better ones. Maybe a change of bedding altogether. He tended to go for dark colors, but Cora needed light around her. She needed things that were beautiful. Her apartment had shown that.

He filled a glass with cold water and set it on the nightstand in case she was thirsty. He felt like he was all thumbs waiting for her to finish her bath, but he didn't want to rush her. Sitting down on the edge of the bed facing the bathroom door in case she needed him, he checked his phone.

No messages from King. One interoffice email from Nadia stating the afternoon appointment complained of someone calling her and hanging up. Cora was the closest; she was going to be surprised by her take from the pool. He'd already fronted her ante so she would hopefully be happy.

Van doubled-checked his security system through his phone. Everything was locked up tight, no alarms or sensors tripped.

Van looked up to see the bathroom door still

partially closed. He could hear the water lapping in the tub, but there was no other sound. He started doing some online shopping, thinking of things his mate might want or need. He put in an order for all the items he could remember from her bathroom and kitchen. He wanted it to be as easy for her to settle into her new home as it was in her old one.

After a while the door in front of him cracked open, the dimmed light from the bathroom filtering into the bedroom. Cora was silhouetted in the light, wrapped in a large white bath towel.

"Van?"

"I'm here. You all done?"

She took a step forward, her voice was sleepy when she said, "I was falling asleep in the tub. I didn't want to drown."

"I wouldn't have let that happen," Van said with a smile.

She smiled back, "I know you wouldn't."

"You ready for bed?" he asked.

He saw her hesitate, her lower lip between her teeth. "I..."

"Anything, sweets. You know that."

Cora looked up to him and let the towel drop to the floor. Her long hair had been up during her bath and now it flowed around her like a cloud.

Van didn't bother to look away. He drank in her

beauty. He could not have created a more perfect woman.

"Baby?"

"I can't lie next to you all night and not touch you. I'm okay, I don't need more time."

"Cora, you do. We have time. I know you must be tired."

"I am. I'm so tired that if I try to go to sleep right now, I'll lie awake thinking of all the ways my life has crashed and burned around me. I don't want to think right now. I want to make a choice that I know in my heart is the right one."

"You know there is no turning back, right? You'll be marked by me. Any birth control you're on won't stop a pregnancy."

"I understand. I'm willing to leave that up to fate. It brought you into my life. And I'm glad that it did. I didn't know that I needed you. But now I see it. Isn't it funny? It's almost as if I missed you before I knew you."

Van stood up and walked towards her, getting into her space, his hands sliding around her smooth hips. "You may have missed me, but I've been waiting for you just as long."

There wasn't any reason to wait. Van knew of other couples that had waited too long and it caused fights among other Kindred. Their animals not feeling secure in their claim and willing to fight others to establish it.

"I know. Please don't make me wait," Cora said, her eyes pleading with him.

Van kissed her, pouring all of his heart into it. Reaching down, he picked her up and carried her to the bed. He laid her out in the middle and stepped back. He didn't ever want to forget the way she looked in that moment.

Stripping out of his clothes, he joined her in the bed and started running his hands over her body. He traced her collarbone, her shoulders, all the way down to her fingertips. He kissed the palm of each hand and then placed a kiss in the middle of her chest. Her heartbeat was like a drum in his ears.

She was breathing fast, every rise and fall of her chest, pushing her tight pink nipples towards him. The light shining in through the windows made her pale skin glow. He cupped each breast, his tanned skin contrasting with paleness. He kissed and sucked the taut peak into his mouth. Her hands threaded through his hair.

"Van," she gasped.

He liked that. He liked his name on her lips. It made the animal inside him proud.

Van moved his hands down her body as he continued to suck her swollen mounds into his mouth. He found the short nest of curls at her apex and teased his fingers lightly over the top.

"Open for me," he urged.

Her legs slid open and he let his fingers slide down to the wet center of her. She was slick with need and his cock that was already hard, flexed against his belly.

Van knew he was big and he wanted to make sure that their first time together was nothing but pleasure. Circling her opening, he dipped his fingers inside her. She was tight and luscious. He added another finger and spread them to test if she was ready.

"Van," she moaned. "I can't wait, please don't tease me, honey."

Leaving his hand right where it was, he brought his mouth to hers. He kissed her hard. "Sweets, when I'm teasing you, you'll know. I just want to make sure you're ready for me."

"I'm ready, I'm so ready," she moaned.

Van liked that she didn't want to wait. He'd been hard for her since yesterday, and he already thought he'd passed the point of needing to prove his resolve.

Leaning back, he pulled away from her heat and wrapped his hands around her thighs. He spread her wide, taking in the beauty of her. He wanted to see every moment, wanted to savor it. Letting his cock fall between her legs, he stared, just for a moment. Then his vision blurred as Cora's hand came down to wrap around his cock and guide him to her entrance.

"Van, I'm yours," she said.

It was an offering that he had never hoped to experience. She was wholeheartedly choosing him. It was humbling and made him proud as hell at the same time.

As the end of his cock slid into her tight pussy, he forced himself to keep his eyes open. He wanted to close them and let the sensation wash over him but he didn't. He fought to watch every inch of himself disappear inside her.

He took in the view of them fused together, one body. She was squeezing his cock tight and when he looked up, her eyes were on him. They held an emotion he wasn't brave enough to name. There was hope as she looked at him and it made him want to be everything she needed.

"I claim you, Cora Butler. You are now part of my life and my clan."

She smiled so sweetly back at him he felt it like a punch in the gut.

He started to move, ensuring she was with him at every moment. He touched her, caressed and kissed her body. He brought her to a fevered pitch knowing she would be the first to come and if he did his job right the second to come also.

"Van, honey, please," she said, her body bucking up against him.

Van reached between them and pressed his fingers against her swollen clit, rubbing it to bring her orgasm crashing down. Her pussy pulsed around his cock as her nails dragged down his back.

The low growl that came out of Van echoed through the room, his inner animal loving the ferocity of her response. He wanted her aggressive and passionate.

"Damn, you're good."

She gave him a smile. "You're easy to please. Especially when you're doing most of the work."

"You'll get your turn," he promised.

Van couldn't wait any longer. He grabbed her hips and rolled her over, pulling her up to her knees.

Cora didn't seem to mind as she flipped her hair over her shoulder and looked back at him. Her look was one of pure desire.

He didn't wait, he slid his cock back into her and moved into her with an urgency to bring them both to their climax. He listened to her moans and gasps as they urged him on. Those noises meant he was doing it right; he was bringing his mate pleasure. His pleasure was a given. There was no way that this wasn't going to be the best experience of his life.

Van wished he could have brought her to her climax over and over before coming, but this time was about claiming her, not dragging out his desires.

He could feel himself building; he needed her to come with him. It was important.

Reaching around between her leg, he found that sensitive bundle of nerves and rubbed it with the pads of his fingers. She was pushing her hips back against his, meeting every thrust in an almost violent crash, their flesh moving together, both with the same goal.

"Cora, now sweets, come for me."

Cora let out a keening sound and her pussy clamped down on his cock, squeezing him and bringing his orgasm to a peak. It hit him like a ton of bricks; his head flew back as he roared. His body jerked and he felt the hot cum jet out of him. He gripped her hips as he jerked his seed into her, marking her as his forever.

A tethering connection formed between them. He could feel the link to her soul connecting with his. It was strong like iron, forged in loved from him to her.

Cora had stopped moving under him. Her body was frozen, her muscles tense and locked. He knew she had come, he had felt it pour over his cock. Now she wasn't moving and he was starting to worry.

"Baby?" he said, pulling her body upright bringing them both to their knees. He wrapped his arms around her and gently kissed her neck, his cock still deep inside her. He wanted to make sure not a drop of him left her yet.

"Are you okay?" he asked.

Her head had fallen back against his chest. She didn't say anything to him, but instead dragged one of his hands up over to cover her heart.

The skin there was hot, almost pulsing under his palm. It took him a moment to realize that his Kindred mark was pulsing to.

He turned her in his arms, not caring that their connection had been broken, and looked down at her chest. Right over her heart was the same symbol he'd carried from birth. Hers was glistening, as though it was lit from inside her, the colors of the rainbow shimmering over the design.

"Cora..." he said, his voice catching. He really hoped that this sudden moment of weakness happened to all the badass Kindred he knew, and not just him. Because it was the most beautiful thing he had ever seen.

"I can feel you," she breathed, her eyes big with wonder.

Van leaned his forehead against hers. The world's most precious person was right there in his arms.

"You're mine now," he said to her and the words were more than a promise.

"And you're mine. I can't believe how fast my life has changed, but I don't regret it for a second. This was right, it was meant to be. I get it now."

Van kissed her soft and slow, his mate deserved soft and slow and Van took the rest of the evening to show her just how much he loved her.

CHAPTER 21

Cora couldn't stop staring at her mark. She'd gotten up in the middle of the night in between the two other love making sessions Van had initiated, to use the bathroom. He seemed insatiable, and she couldn't help but be flattered.

In the bathroom she looked into the mirror, not even bothering to take in her messy hair and kiss swollen lips. Her eyes instead went straight to her heart. That Celtic looking infinity symbol was tattooed into her skin with iridescent ink. Something she'd only seen briefly on other Kindred mates... and now she had one of her own. It was like a shining beacon that declared her mate's claim on her.

She understood why people showed them off. It

meant so much more than a just a sign that two people were together. It was a sign of permanent commitment that could never be pawned or given away. You wanted to show it off.

The moment that Van had come inside her she had felt different. Her body had changed; it adjusted, for lack of a better word. She could feel the entire framework of her biology move into another state. She knew that the connection she had with him was permanent, and it brought her a sense of peace. As she looked up to her own eyes staring back at her, she saw that the bruise on her face was almost gone, the pain having slipped away without her noticing. A Kindred perk for sure. But perks aside, there was something else she was feeling that outshone everything else.

She would never be alone again.

After curling back into his arms, she was able to get a short nap before he woke her again. She guessed it was just this first night with him. He couldn't possibly keep this up every day, could he?

Waking up alone the next morning, she had a moment of worry that it had all been an amazing, sexy dream, but when she stretched she found all the lovely aches and sweet sore spots that told her it had all been real.

Getting up, she made her way to the walk-in shower and took the world's fastest shower. Her hair needed washing so she used Van's all-in-one shampoo, eww. Clean hair was worth it in this case. Drying off, she wandered into the closet to see if she could borrow something from Van and found her suitcase laid out, unzipped on the floor.

Grabbing a set of bra and panties, she found a long-sleeve sweater dress and pair of Capri leggings that looked comfortable. She also found one of her favorite scarves and made herself a headband to cover her wet messy bun.

Putting on mascara, eyeliner, and some gloss, she walked out into the living area. Her eyes went to the kitchen and found a shirtless Van standing over the stove.

She wanted to play it cool. She wanted to be fine with this morning after routine. Not like she had been completely destroyed and rebuilt by her evening with Van.

She wasn't able to be cool.

His eyes came up from the pan he was poking with a spatula and they narrowed into a look of pure lust.

Cora went from casual face to huge goofy grin. She took off running and Van was able to drop the spatula just at the moment she took a leaping jump into his arms. She wrapped her arms and legs around his body and squeezed. She loved how strong he was, how his muscles circled her and held her like she weighed nothing.

"Morning, Cora," he said, his voice husky.

The way he said her name was like a caress. It tickled her skin and made her want to wiggle against him.

"Good morning," she said shyly into his neck.

"How do you feel?"

Cora thought that wasn't an easy question at all. "Different," she finally said, hoping that it encompassed enough of her feelings.

Van grunted. "Hungry?"

"Starved," she said pushing her face into his neck and breathing him in. He'd showered too, and even though they had used the same soap and shampoo, he smelled much yummier than she did.

"Then park your ass wherever you want and I'll bring you food."

Cora let herself slide down the front of him, making sure as much of their body parts touched as possible.

"Sweets, really?" Van asked, a twinkle in his eye.

She could feel that he was hard and it made her body react, her nipples pebbling against her bra.

"It's your fault. You gave me a taste, now I want more."

"Let's eat first and I'll see what I can do," he said, giving her ass a slap.

Cora looked around the room. There was no formal table and chairs but there were options, the couch, the futon area, or the counter facing him.

She chose to spend her valuable time staring at Van. She took a seat at the counter and leaned over the edge to see what he was cooking.

"What are we having?"

"Protein, you drained me last night."

"Hah, like that was my doing," she scoffed.

Van stopped what he was doing to give her a heated look. "It had everything to do with you, trust me. That ass, those tits, forget about it."

"Tits, you're so gross," she said laughing.

Van just smiled at her. He knew she wasn't serious. She sat and watched him move around the kitchen, stirring and chopping. He looked at home in front of the stove.

Orange juice and coffee were deposited on the counter and she wrapped her hands around the coffee cup gratefully. Finally a steaming plate of eggs, bacon, and fresh cut melon were set in front of her. A plate of English muffins was also added, the melted butter dripping off them.

"Sorry, this was as brunch-like as I could get," Van said taking his seat next to her.

"Ahh, you tried to make me brunch. That's sweet," she said.

"It's not sweet, it's what mates do."

"Well, I still think it's nice."

Van grunted. "Good."

"So, what's the plan today?" she asked, taking a bite of salty crunchy bacon.

"As long as I don't get called in by King, I thought we could spend it here. I'm sure you'd like to get some of your things moved in. You'll need me for the heavy lifting."

Now it was Cora's turn to grunt. "I should probably make some calls to the boards I'm on. They may no longer be needing my services."

"Why the fuck not?"

"Because, I was on them when my last name was going to be Dillard. They may not feel the need to keep me around anymore. Which makes me sad. I liked what I did. I know it was volunteer, but it was still work."

"I've got calls to make myself. I need to contact our Clan Head and inform him of our new member. I can ask at the same time if there are any openings in our business charities. They always need help. It would be good for you to get to know some people too."

"I like working with kids. That's a passion of mine."

"I don't see why you can't continue that. Although, I'd prefer you took a week or two to get your bearings. Recover from what you went through, adjust to us," he said.

"You said bear-ings," she giggled.

Van shook his head at her and smirked. He gave her a knowing look that told her he thought she was adorable. They finished breakfast and Van made her a second cup of coffee after she insisted on cleaning up.

She tidied the kitchen while Van started bringing boxes in. They hadn't had time to label everything, so it was a surprise every time they opened something. She left all of her kitchen things in boxes. Waiting to see if there were specific items that she would need and could add to Van's kitchen.

As she found her treasures, she lovingly looked over them. Some were from her childhood, heart shaped stones she'd found on a family trip to the beach. A blown glass paperweight that had a floating sea turtle inside. She'd met the artist during a street fair in Fremont. They were items that had moved her in some way, but now she hesitated. Would Van want these things in his space?

Then again, he'd said it was *her* space from the beginning. She already carried his mark; a few knick-knacks were probably not the end of the world.

Cora moved around the room, finding just the right corner, or shelf to add her favorite things. Van's space almost felt like an empty canvas, just waiting for someone to add some color.

Her favorite purple cable knit throw was tossed casually over the back of the couch, and by casual she meant moved and tweaked until it looked effortlessly thrown.

Unpacking another box, she found a hand woven basket she'd bought from a man selling them from the back of his van in a parking lot. He had been sitting on the bumper, a half finished basket between his legs. Cora had watched his hands fly over the fibers as the basket came to life.

Now it sat at the end of the couch, more of her blankets and throws piled inside it. She found herself smiling. She knew these things would be loved here, if not just by her, but by Van because he knew they meant something to her. That made her heart sing.

Putting her clothes away in that beautiful closet was almost as good as Christmas morning. She had so much space at her disposal that she started to get fancy by color coordinating her things. She felt a little silly putting her inexpensive jewelry in the display case, but it still looked nice. Anytime she had needed something nicer, Chaz would borrow something from his mother. It was always a big deal and even after years of the same routine, she had to listen to the rules of the jewelry. Cora had never stolen, lost, or misplaced anything. That did make her think of her evening gowns. She didn't see a lot of need for those in the future. She'd have to consider donating them.

Van didn't seem bored watching her get settled; in fact, he looked content to just be with her. She loved that.

He did excuse himself to make his calls and when he returned he looked a little chagrined.

"Are you okay?" she asked, not used to seeing him look at all uncomfortable.

"Yeah, our Clan Head was just very excited to hear about you. He was on his way to tell my parents, which means that call is coming soon. They'll want to video chat so they can see you," he warned.

"I need to do something with my hair!" Cora gasped and jumped up from the floor of the closet and headed toward the bathroom. She ran back to the closet to grab her hair dryer and makeup from her bags and then locked herself in the bathroom.

※

Van had watched Cora move around the loft. At first her footsteps were hesitant, not sure the extent to which she should co-mingle their belongings.

Not wanting to pressure her, he sat back and let her find her place. It was there, and his patience paid off when she found it for herself. Her face would light up as she found something in the bottom of a box and then she would spin excitedly, her eyes scanning for the perfect place to display the treasure.

The more things she added, the happier Van felt. His mate was feathering their nest. Or in this case, feathering their den. She was adding beauty and comfort to every corner of their life. Van could feel his heart warming as he watched. For the longest time, this place had been where he slept and ate. It wasn't a refuge. Until now, he had only felt that kind of peace when he was shifted and allowed to run in the woods.

Now Cora was there and she was the reason his loft was transforming into a home. He could feel it, almost taste it. She was spreading her love, her softness, on everything. There would never be a time again that he wouldn't want to come home. From now on she would be there, worrying about him, eager to see him.

There would be food, laughter, and love every time they were together. He couldn't believe how lucky he was. This precious woman was saving him from a life half lived. She was making him whole.

CHAPTER 22

C ora finished with her makeup and hair just in time for Van to tell her that he had gotten a warning text from his dad that they were going to call.

Van led her up to his office. The room was in between his gym and spare room so it had no windows. There was recessed lighting spread over the ceiling that made the whole room glow in natural light.

There was a large desk facing the door with a number of computer monitors spread over it. To the side was a drafting style table that held a set of building plans.

Van pointed her towards a big leather chair and grabbed a spare chair to pull up next to her.

"What should I know about them?"

Van sat next to her and turned on the computer. "My mom, Eileen, is Kindred. My dad, Simon, is human. They've been mated for almost forty years, I'm the oldest then my sister came next. They love being grandparents so I apologize in advance for anything they might say."

"What if they don't like me?"

Van couldn't believe she could think that for even a minute. "They'll love you because I do. They know that my future holds nothing but happiness because of you. How could any parent want to ruin that?"

"Well, maybe they wouldn't ruin it on purpose, but accidently. You haven't met my parents yet. They may take you around the neighborhood to introduce you as their new Kindred son-in-law. Oh crap, now that I say it, that's exactly what they would do," she groaned.

"Then I get to meet the neighbors. Remember, you get to meet my entire clan. It's a little more of a show than just your parents being excited."

"Like how much of a show? I don't have to stand up in front of a bunch of people do I?"

He wanted to lie; the look on her face told him she wasn't thrilled. "Haven't you given speeches for your charities before?"

"That's different! People weren't there to see *me*. They didn't even want to hear my speech. It was about the open bar," she admitted.

"This is going to be fine. If you want to start small, I can do that. Just immediate family and, of course, the two Original Families."

"Original Families?"

"Original Families. My clan has two, which is rare. They are the families that can trace their lineage back as far as the Kindred have records. They were the first families to organize into larger groups. They were the ones that made sure the Kindred had a voice in developing governments. They still often hold key political positions to ensure that our kind are treated fairly."

"Wow, so Kindred dignitaries? They'll want to meet me?"

"Every new clan member is important. They want to make a good impression on you just as much as you will want to them. They need to know that you're going to keep our secrets and work towards our future," Van explained.

"No pressure there," Cora said with a snort.

The computer chimed and Van reached over to hit the keyboard.

Cora's stopped him her hand resting gently on

his. "Give me a second," she said taking a deep breath.

"Baby, you're fine," Van assured her, shaking his head.

"Okay, go ahead."

Cora didn't look ready at all. She looked a little green around the edges.

The connection solidified and Van smiled at his parents as they came into view.

"Mom, Dad, I'd like you to meet my mate, Cora Butler."

Cora waved shyly, "Hi, it's nice to meet you," she said her voice shaking a little.

"Van, why is that woman so nervous? Have you been bossing her around?" his mother barked.

"What? Mom, no, I mean a little, but no," Van started.

"Honey, I'm Eileen. I'm so happy that you're part of the family. Do not, I repeat, *do not* let that big bear boss you around. He thinks he's smarter than everyone else on the planet. You look smart enough to me; you've probably got him figured out all ready."

Cora let out a sharp laugh. Van gave her a sideways glance.

"See, smart girl," his mother said proudly.

Van's father spoke up next. "Son, you couldn't have done better. Hi there, I'm Simon, it's nice to meet you, dear. Although, do I detect a black eye? What the hell is that about?"

His mother leaned closer to the screen. "Van of Clan Rekkr, you let your mate get a black eye! Where were you? Why didn't you watch her better?"

"Mom, calm down, this happened before we met. Not much I could have done."

His mother made a harrumphing noise. "Likely story."

"Cora, you're in good hands even if they are big and clumsy," Simon said.

"Wow, so I see how it's going to be," Van said leaning back against his chair.

Cora looked at him, concerned.

He shook his head as he answered. "They already like you better."

"Don't worry, Cora. He's a pouter, has been since he was a cub. Just ignore him, he'll come around," his mother said with an indulgent smile.

"I don't pout," Van said, crossing his arms. He sat there for a moment and then realized what he'd done and unfolded them.

"When is the announcement?" his father asked.

"Elias said I just needed to call. He'd arrange everything," Van answered.

Eileen nodded. "I must say, I wasn't sure he was

going to be as successful as Head of the Clan as he is. He's not even from an Original Family."

"Elias was the best candidate. Besides, if he wasn't good, we could always replace him," Simon stated.

Cora seemed surprised by that. "You can kick out your Clan Heads?"

"With that many Kindred and mates you can't do a bad job without a revolt. We vote our Clan Heads in and every three years we come together to evaluate if they stay in or if we want to change and go in a different direction. We do a 'keep' or 'go' vote and then if it's 'go,' we open it up to candidates. No hard feelings anywhere," Van said.

"That seems fair. If they're doing a great job they don't have to run again," Cora agreed.

"It's worked for thousands of years, don't fix what ain't broke," Simon said in a twangy voice.

"So honey, where are you parents?" Eileen asked.

"Back in Texas. I haven't actually told them about this yet. I need to fill them in on a lot of things."

"I'm sure it will be alright. We would love to meet them. If it's easier, we could fly down and spend some time with them. I mean we *will* be sharing grandchildren soon," Eileen said with a wink.

"Mom, really?"

"Son, your mother got one look at your mate's red hair and she's already dreaming of what the new babies will look like," his father laughed.

"Good lord," Cora said, blushing.

"Sorry, I tried to warn you," Van reminded her.

They continued chatting for a while. They grilled Cora on every topic under the sun, and she seemed to relax as they went along. His parents never stopped smiling, so that probably helped to ease her tension.

His parents were happy, over the moon. Both of their children were mated and that was the most they could have hoped for. He knew that they wanted the best for him and knew that he'd finally found it.

After an hour they signed off with promises to call in a few days. Cora asked to use his office to make some calls herself. He excused himself, knowing that she didn't need an audience for those conversations, but he stayed close and kept an ear out in case she needed him.

He called in lunch from a teriyaki place he knew delivered. He had it waiting for her when she finally came down.

Without looking at him, she flopped on the

couch and pulled a pillow over her face.

"Sweets?"

"Ugh, ugh, ugh, that was torture," she moaned muffled into the pillow.

"So?"

"So, I'm unemployed. Not one of the charities wanted to keep me on. They said they could find a replacement and thanked me for my service to the organizations. It was all very civil, like chopping someone's head off with an axe. Clean and painful."

"Like I said, we can get you a new job," Van said. He carried over the containers of food and set them down. "Beer?"

"Yes, please," she said weakly, dropping the pillow.

Van retrieved the beers and sat next to her. "I'm sorry. I know it wasn't the outcome you wanted."

"You know, it wasn't but," she said, taking a swig of the beer, "I'm realizing that it would have connected me to my past, and I would have had to look at Chaz' mother at every meeting. I don't want anything to do with that life. I want my future."

Van leaned over and kissed her. "That's what I want to hear."

Opening one of the take-out containers, he handed it to her with a fork.

"Mmm, teriyaki, I love this stuff. What's in the

third box?" she asked.

"More teriyaki, one isn't enough for me."

Van tucked into his food. He wanted to comfort her, but he knew it would take time. She'd been through a lot and her life was still going to change.

Cora had taken a number of bites then paused, setting her box in her lap. She stared off into space for moment then Van watched her reach up to her mate mark. Just the top of it was visible in the dress she was wearing. Her fingers trailed over the edge of the design.

He watched her for a few moments.

"You know I can feel that," he said to her.

Her eyes shot to his, "Really?" Her hand dropped away from the mark.

"Watch," he said bringing his own hand up to his mark, he pulled the neck of his black shirt down to expose the symbol. He touched it and watched her eyes get bigger.

"It takes a little while for the connection to build. You can always let me know you're alive by touching it. I can do the same for you."

Cora looked down and when she looked back up at him, she had tears in her eyes.

"You don't know how much I needed that. To know that," she said.

"I get it, sweets, I do."

CHAPTER 23

Cora made the call to her parents. They were happy to hear from her, and overjoyed that she was rid of the 'Texas-sized douche,' as they liked to call him. For years they had barely tolerated him, maintaining civility for her sake. They spent the better part of a half hour telling her all the ways they thought that he was a shithead. As though she didn't know all of it already.

They loved the idea of Van's family visiting; they wanted to do a Texas-style party to welcome Van. She loved her parents and she loved that they had so easily accepted her change of situation and the fact that she wanted to be with Van.

Her parents assured her that there wasn't any reason to doubt what was going on. She was smart and had always had a good head on her shoulders. Molly and Patrick Butler wouldn't tell their daughter lies, even though they'd dragged out that Santa Claus thing for way too long.

Cora went to bed that night after an afternoon of unpacking and lovemaking. Van took every opportunity to steal a kiss and hold her tight and she soaked up every touch. As well as mentally, his touch made her feel better physically, her aches and pains were gone. As if they were wiped away by his bold caresses. He touched her like he wanted, but in a way that she was sure he knew would make her burn for him

Some of those kisses and touches came without any conversation. Just an explosion of intensity that left her reeling, leaning against a wall or counter. He would walk away with a shit-eating grin on his face knowing he'd just spun her.

She was now laying in bed next to him, Van having fallen asleep next to her after making her come twice. It wasn't like she was totally stupid. It wasn't just the passion of a new relationship. She also had the distinct feeling that he was trying to get her pregnant.

The thought had never occurred to her before. It certainly wasn't as though she'd thought about having children with Chaz. It should have at least once popped into her head. Maybe her mind was telling her that it would be a colossally terrible idea. That to bring a child into that relationship would have been cruel, but having a baby with Van wouldn't be cruel. She could already imagine him holding a tiny baby and protecting it will all the fierceness he put into everything he did.

After only one day in his world and she felt different. She felt safer. There wasn't any reason to be afraid or nervous any longer. The thought surprised her. She hadn't seen herself as nervous or afraid before, but that was just the way she'd forced herself to live, to survive.

Although spending another day, locked up cozy in the loft sounded like a nice idea. She knew that he had to get back to work. It was what he did, and she wanted him happy. That thought made her mark tingle. Her connection to him was growing by the minute. It was so profound that if she thought about it too long, she'd start to cry.

That was stupid, crying over something like that. But the fact was she'd been so starved of any real emotions for so long, that it was overwhelming to accept what was coming to her.

Curling into his heat, she let herself drift off, actually looking forward to the next day.

The next morning she wasn't woken by hot

kisses and fingers in her panties. No, this morning it was a smack on the ass and wet kiss on her lips that made her open her eyes.

"Baby, get up, we need to go to the office," Van said, leaning over the bed.

She looked up at him with blurry eyes to see that he was already showered and dressed in his usual black fatigues.

"What? Why?"

"King needs me and I don't want to leave you alone here."

"Van, I'm perfectly safe here. You store valuable things in the warehouse. If that stuff is safe, I'll be safe."

Van went into the closet and came out with clothes, tossing them next to her on the bed. "Here, get dressed. Sweets, I need my mind on the game today and I need you where I know you're safe. Just do this for me, yeah?"

Cora didn't want to be a cranky bitch, but she would have preferred to keep sleeping.

"No shower?"

"No, you're claimed, I don't care who smells you," he said.

"Van, that is so unappealing to a human, just so you know. Nobody wants to think they smell, let alone of sex."

Van looked at her like she was crazy and then shrugged his shoulders. "Get a move on, I'm warming up the car."

Cora watched him leave then jumped out of bed. She managed to hit the bathroom and brush her hair and teeth before scoffing at the items Van had picked out for her to wear and disappearing to the closet. She came out wearing a pair of jeans, her favorite strappy sandals and a gray shirt with a cropped bright red hoodie over top.

Before Van, an outfit as casual as this wasn't anything that she'd normally go out in. But hanging out at the office didn't exactly require a ball gown.

She made a dash to the garage and found Van in the low yellow car, her door open for her. She jumped in and he handed her an insulated mug of coffee.

"Oh, thank goodness," she moaned as she sipped the hot brew.

"I got you, baby," he replied as he put the car into reverse.

They flew through Seattle, and Cora barely bothered to look up. It was easier on her nerves if she didn't. When she did, she felt like she was in a video game where if you almost hit pedestrians you got extra points. So she just kept her head down and tried not to think about how fast they were going, or how many cars Van dodged as they did it.

Arriving at the office, she tried to keep up as Van jumped out when he parked and opened her door for her. They both raced to the elevator and hit the button.

When the doors opened into the lobby Van took off at a jog calling back over his shoulder, "Nadia will set you up!"

Cora looked over to Nadia and smiled. "Hey."

Nadia was shaking her head at Van's back. "Always in a hurry. Like they still don't have to travel."

"Travel?"

"They have to head north; they've got at least an hour before they hit their target."

"Target?" Cora asked, terribly intrigued.

"Sorry, classified. You'll have to ask Van later," she said primly. She didn't look comfortable relaying even that little bit of information, so Cora didn't push her.

Nadia took her to the recovery room. "Van asked that I order in some breakfast for you. There's also a laptop there if you want. The password is 'guest.' There are movies on there or streaming, it's all on the main desktop."

Cora looked around and it felt like she had been

here weeks ago instead of days. "When will they be back?"

Nadia gave her a wry smile. "If I knew that I'd never get overtime. And just a tip, I always get over-time. If you need anything, just let me know."

Cora nodded. She had a feeling it was going to be a long day.

Before Van left, he came into the room and kissed her as though he was going away to war. It was scary, this first time he was going away to work. She didn't know what was going on and she didn't feel it was her place to ask. He was dressed with a thick vest covered in knives, guns, and other items she couldn't readily identify.

"Be careful," she said.

"Don't worry about me, I have a reason to come back," he replied.

"I know you can handle yourself, but I'm going to worry anyway."

Van kissed her again and left. She felt the loss of his presence. She ate her pancakes and drank her coffee while she checked her email. It was light considering she was no longer getting the charity emails that normally dictated her life.

There was an email from her parents already asking about dates for visits. A few emails from her credit cards, which she knew she was going to have to take care of at some point. And then there was an urgent message waiting at the top. One that she dreaded opening. She didn't have to. She could just leave it there and not bother.

Instead, she opened it. It was from Chaz's mother. It was a scathing diatribe of how ungrateful Cora was. How she had let down the whole family, a family that had invested in her future. That it had all been a waste because she was a selfish brat who had run off with someone who was no better than an animal.

Cora could take all of that. She didn't care how it much it hurt. She *had* let them down, but she wasn't so naive to believe that the family wouldn't rebound as though she had never been there.

But it wasn't that part that made her want to throw the laptop across the room. It was the fact she called Van an *animal*.

That woman could go fuck herself.

Cora realized that there was no reason to worry about anything the Dillard's had to say ever again. They weren't worth her time. She realized now that she was worth more. She deserved a man that loved her. And she deserved to have a future that actually took her happiness into account.

Deleting the email, she made sure to delete it from her trash folder and from her cloud service.

There was no reason to keep that around any longer to look at again.

She wasn't going to cry, they didn't get her tears. Cora found a movie and started it. *Tiger's Heart*, it was one of her favorite Kindred and human romances. Now she could see it through a different set of eyes and she connected with the heroine like she never had before. She played another once that one was over, falling asleep at the romantic climax as the Kindred claimed his mate.

CHAPTER 24

When she woke she wasn't sure what time it was. She wandered out to the front desk but Nadia wasn't there. The computer was still on, as were the lights, so she knew that the receptionist hadn't left her alone. Glancing around the desk she saw an opened box. When she looked inside she found her purse. Flipping over to see where it came from she saw that it was from the motel she'd been staying at and was addressed to Van.

He'd gotten her purse back. She looked inside and found her money, all her credit cards and ID. Nothing was missing. Deciding it would be a nice thing to do; she grabbed her purse and wrote a note to Nadia letting her know she was going to go grab dinner for both of them.

It was the least she could do. Nadia might have had plans for the evening. A husband, a boyfriend, she wasn't sure. Cora knew she worked hard and she put up with Van and the other guys. From what she saw, it couldn't be easy.

Signing the note, she headed over to the elevator. She pressed the button for the lobby and waited. There was no sound like the elevator was moving. Then she remembered Van's keycard. Turning around she went back to Nadia's desk and looked to see if there was a spare. How else did clients leave? Cora bent over to look in one of the drawers when she saw a small white button under the lip of the desk that had a small label by it that said 'Lobby' she took a chance and pressed it. Hearing the elevator's motor whir to life she ran over as the doors opened and got in. She'd never even seen the lobby of the building but odds were it would kick her out on the street.

The doors opened and she stepped into a generic unmanned lobby. She could see out the windows that it was almost dusk. The doors closed behind her with a click as she stepped out onto the street. Cora spun around, shit, how was she supposed to get back in? Cora decided she'd go through the garage and use the intercom in the basement by the elevator she'd seen when Van took her up the first time. She'd only be gone for fifteen minutes at most. Cora didn't think there was any big worry now that she was with Van. A dinner run didn't need back-up from armed professionals. Cora took a deep breath, trying to feel confident in her plans. It would be fine. Everything would be fine. Better to beg forgiveness than ask permission, right? The crowds on the street had thinned as the work day ended and people made their way back home or out for the evening.

As soon as she was out on the sidewalk she looked up and down the street. The building sat in the middle of the block and once she got her bearings, she figured out there was a fantastic burrito truck usually parked on the corner a few blocks up.

Zipping up her hoodie she started off down the street. She kept her head down and started the fast march that she saved for busy city streets. It was safer to not make eye contact and to get where you were going.

She was focusing so hard at putting one foot in front of the other, that she missed the black SUV that was following her down the road. When she stopped for a crosswalk, the SUV pulled up to the curb and the door flew open.

Cora still didn't realize what was happening until an iron grip circled her arm and she was tugged violently to the side. She found herself staring up at black tinted windows as she caught a glimpse of a man wearing a ski mask and dark glasses.

The door was slamming shut before she could scream. But she did scream at least once, she also kicked and lashed out. The man pinned her down easily and she felt something being pulled over her head, blocking her vision.

"Go!" the man barked. "And, you, scream all you want. No one is going to hear you."

Cora's hands were pulled together as she continued trying to kick and scream. Something tightened around her wrists and she could no longer lash out. Her legs were kicking, trying to make contact with anything she could. She thought she might have gotten a few blows in before her ankles were secured.

"Let me go!"

"Sorry, can't do that. You might as well enjoy the ride," she heard the voice say. From what she remembered of her last kidnapping, these guys were professionals compared to Frick and Frack. These guys were something else.

Cora stopped screaming, she knew that the kidnapper was right. What she couldn't wrap her head around was who these guys were. How do you get kidnapped twice in a week? Was she a magnet for this kind of thing now?

She also felt like a prize idiot. She'd left the safety and security of the office. Van put her there so he wouldn't worry about her. He wanted her there so she could be protected. What did she do? She had wandered outside, by herself, at dusk. It happened so quickly that if anyone was asked about what they'd seen, they would have a hard time giving any clear facts about the car or her captors. Damn these generic cars.

Van was going to be pissed at her for sure for taking such a stupid risk. Though in her defense, she didn't think that the Kristanzi family would try again so soon. If they didn't get any money out of Chaz the first time, what made them think this time would be any different?

Unless it wasn't them. How many people had Chaz ticked off? That was a loaded question, he was a dick and nobody really liked him. They pretended to, but rarely did anyone keep the disdain out of their eyes when talking to him.

So was it someone else? Did this have to do with Van? How could anyone even know about her yet?

Trying out her captors, she kicked out her foot and got a punch in the gut for her efforts. The pain shocked her as the air whooshed out of her lungs. She couldn't hold back the moan as her stomach flexed against the pain.

"Settle the fuck down," the man growled at her.

That was a terrible test and one she wasn't going to repeat. Violence was definitely on the menu with these guys.

She wanted to raise her hand to her mark. She wanted to at least have that connection with Van, if only for a moment. But she was afraid the man would think she was messing with her hood and didn't want to get hit again. There was coldness around her mate mark. It was probably all in her head, but it felt that way. She knew they were driving her away from the city, but in her heart, it felt like they were trying to drive her away from Van.

As the SUV bounced along, she leaned against the door on the opposite side of the seat from the man who had punched her. In those crucial first few moments she had been too focused on screaming and fighting against her captors that she hadn't been paying attention to the turns the vehicle had taken. But she had no idea what direction they were going. After a while she also lost track of time. The two men in the car didn't talk.

They were that good. Talking gave things away. Frick and Frack talked a lot, but they had been stupid. These guys were anything but stupid.

After what seemed like forever, the vehicle came to a stop. She was dragged roughly from the car and thrown unceremoniously over one of the goon's shoulders. Her stomach cramped painfully as his shoulder hit her in the gut and she knew there would be a bruise there later.

Fear coursed through her. This time was so much different than the last. There was real fear in her heart that she might not make it out of this. What would that mean for Van? What happened to Kindred when they lost their mates? It was another one of those secrets that wasn't talked about much. With the older ones it didn't seem to affect them any differently than humans. Missing the chance at a long life together was always painful. But Van, he had a long life ahead of him. Could he find someone else? Was that even possible? Were there backup mates?

That wasn't a good sign that she was thinking that way. Van needed her to survive this, she was sure of that more than anything else.

CHAPTER 25

Van was crouched in the dark, his body pressed against the side of the fancy house in the Medina section of Seattle. He'd been there for hours, waiting.

One of their high profile clients had received a credible threat to his family. King Security was always on call for clients that kept them on retainer. Family protection was a service they offered, even if that meant something as simple as driving the kids to school to make sure they were safe.

King didn't want the perpetrators to get away this time. These particular thugs had been harassing his client for long enough, and he wanted it done and over with. The family deserved that peace of mind.

KSI had been monitoring them for a number of months. Driving the children to school, assessing the threat. Nothing had surface as a visible or verifiable threat until tonight.

The device in Van's ear chirped to life and King's harsh whisper demanded, "Report."

"Negative," Van responded.

"Negative," Anson replied.

Luca was next, "Negative and freezing my balls off."

Van smiled into the dark. Luca was just fucking around. That man had spent days perched in a tree to get a single shot off. Cold didn't bother him.

A much more feminine voice came in next. "My balls are frozen too." Eden was one of the team that had been on another assignment, guarding the Queen of Pop, Bliss Hartley, which was an exhausting assignment. King wanted her to have some down time, but right now, they needed all hands on deck.

King's annoyed voice came on, "Eden, report, and not on your balls."

"Negat....wait," there was a pause. "Subject on east perimeter. Dressed in black, alone."

Van was instantly alert. His muscles were starting to cramp and he wanted to stretch, but he didn't want to give up his position. After Eden, he was the next closest to the perp.

"Confirm we have single target," King broke in.

Van peered through the dark, seeing the silhouette of a man, a human, moving through the shadows. "I see one, on my side. He's coming in fast," he said quickly, confirming Eden's visual.

"Engage," King ordered.

Van took a step out of the shadows and made it halfway to the man before the perp saw him coming. The moment he realized he wasn't alone, the man turned and raised a gun. Van's arm came up with his own weapon and a shot rang out.

The man stopped where he was standing and the last thing Van's saw was the man crumbling to the ground. And then everything exploded with white light, and the ground rushed up toward his face as he fell into darkness.

Van could hear things before he could see anything.

"Van, shift! You have to shift now!"

He thought that was King's voice he heard, it sounded like him. But he couldn't remember his boss and friend ever sounding so urgent.

"Stop fucking around, Van, shift!" That sounded like Luca. He sounded concerned too. That was even more confusing.

Van hurt, his whole body felt like it was on fire. There was a pain under his arm and in his chest. The pain radiated through to his heart and it was confusing. There was also a wet feeling; like he'd fallen in a puddle. He could tell his vest was gone because someone was holding something under his arm.

Cracking an eye open he found King and Luca leaning over him. He saw King raise a knife and heard cloth tearing.

"Shift, *now!*" King ordered.

Van's mind started ticking over a little faster, the fuzziness wearing off. The pain meant that he was hurt, but he wasn't sure how, but it was bad enough that King's face was angry.

He could feel himself getting dizzy again, his vision blurring. With the last bit of strength he had, he shifted under their hands.

His aching skin felt like it was tearing apart as his animal morphed out of his human frame. The growth of his bones and the sprouting of hair normally wasn't a painful experience. This time every inch of his body resisted.

As his bear shape fully formed, he could feel the bullet push out of his skin with an aching burst. That was the pain under his arm. The feeling of his lung expanding also made sense now. He'd been shot under the arm. The odds of that happening were slim, but it was still an exposed area.

"Give yourself a minute, let your animal heal," King ordered.

Van wasn't going to argue, his bear was lying on the ground, panting as he felt the majority of his organ heal itself. It was going to be a few days before he could take a deep breath, but he wasn't going to die.

Luca was moving away from him, his hand covered in blood. Van watched through his still blurry gaze as Luca rifled through his ripped clothing. King must have cut them off of him when he was hurt.

Van heard his phone vibrating on the concrete path. There was no way it should be going off while he was on an op. Nadia would never use that number, and he hadn't given it to Cora because she didn't have her phone back yet.

"We've got a problem," Luca said, handing the phone to King.

King read the screen and dialed the number. "Nadia, what the fuck is going on?"

Van raised his giant head and let out a growl. Why would Nadia be calling when she knew where they were?

King's eyes shot to his and Van immediately

shifted back to human form, his body cracking hard as he came back into his skin. Anson was running toward the group, a stack of clothes in his hands. They always kept clothes in all the cars for these situations.

Van nodded as he took the clothes that were handed to him. He was half dressed in the few moments it took King to get an answer to his question.

"Got it," he said hanging up on Nadia. "Cora is missing."

Those words struck right at Van's heart. "How?"

"Nadia went to the bathroom and when she came out, she found a note saying Cora was going to grab dinner for them. Nadia ran after her hoping to stop her before she left the building. When she got to the street she saw some police officers questioning witnesses, and people were saying that a red headed woman was kidnapped off the street."

"Fucking Kristanzi!" Van roared.

"I don't think it's them, they know that well is dry. This has to be something else. Let's get to the truck and pull up the feeds and see what we can get. Anson, you and Eden, stay here and fill in the police. Deal with the client, explain we had to go and I will contact him as soon as we're through," King ordered.

Anson nodded and took off towards the medics

that were working on the man Van had shot. They were prepping him for transport. After that it was the law that would deal with him. Van finished dressing and was pulling on his boots, ignoring the pain in his side as he followed King, who was already moving towards their vehicles.

Pulling open the driver's side door, King jumped in and started typing on the computer that was attached to the dash.

Van leaned into the cab over King's shoulder as the video feeds started popping up. King checked through the feeds trying to see if he could spot anything.

"There," Van said, pointing to the top screen. Just off to the side of the frame, he could see Cora walking, her head down, hands tucked into the pockets of her hoodie. She was looking down, completely unaware that she was being followed.

Van was going to have to give her some lessons on personal safety after all of this was over.

"Recognize the SUV?" King asked.

"No, looks like one of ours, really," Van hissed, watching the door swing open and a masked man pull Cora into the vehicle in just a few seconds. The people on the street didn't really know what they were seeing and he didn't blame them for not interfering. It happened so fast.

"Who the fuck is that," King growled.

"We need to put out feelers. I'll call my contacts, you call yours. Who else might know what's going on?" Van was trying really hard to control himself. Getting angry could come later. He didn't need to lose his focus when his mate was in danger.

This was a professional snatch. These people knew where she was and assumed that she might have been alone. That could have just been a guess. A real organized operation would have people at different potential locations. He wouldn't be surprised if there had been a team at his loft, one at her old apartment, and of course those that waited at the office downtown.

"We can reach out to her ex, I know you don't want that, but it may cut out some dead ends before we waste our time."

"Fine, I'll call him," Van said, his angry rising. If that fucker had anything to do with this, he'd be lucky to live the rest of his life with all his limbs.

His animal wanted to tear and shred and the man wanted to find his mate and lock her up safe. Neither were things he was going to be able to do until he found her.

He didn't know where she was or if she was hurt. The one thing he could do for her in that moment was let her know that she wasn't alone.

Van reached to his mark through the neck of his shirt and covered it with his hand. It warmed to his touch and he hoped she knew that it meant he was coming for her.

CHAPTER 26

Cora strained to hear anything that would give her an idea of where she had been taken, but it was eerily quiet.

As she was carried along, she felt her mate mark warm, and a tingle shot straight to her heart. *Van*.

She almost cried out at the sensation. She didn't know if that was just him telling her he was alive or whether he knew she was missing and was giving her hope. Either way, she knew that he was okay. If he was okay, then he would find her. He would turn the world upside down to get to her; she knew that to the depths of her soul.

The men weren't talking to her, or to each other. She was deposited into a chair. It was a hard affair, no cushy recliner for her. The bindings on her hands were cut and one arm was pulled behind her chair. Taking the opportunity before she lost it, Cora reached up and ran her fingers over her mark. Hopefully the connection worked and Van would know that she was okay and still fighting.

Well, not fighting so much as being trussed up like a chicken. Her hand was ripped away from her mark as someone pulled her hand and tied it behind the chair. What was it with kidnappers liking positions that mangled their captive's shoulders?

Cora was hoping that her legs would be free, but instead they were tied to the legs of the chair after her original restraints were cut. They were making sure she couldn't get away. It also meant that if she struggled too much, she could find herself on the floor with a potential head injury.

There wasn't much she could do but wait and try not to draw anyone's attention.

Cora kept her ears open. There was some movement, and the sound of footsteps. She heard a phone beep, the tapping of fingers over the buttons. Then there was the flick of a lighter, the harsh smoke of a cigarette filling the room.

Keeping her head down as she worked on slowing her breathing. The minutes ticked by and she would start to panic then that warmth over her heart would come back. He knew. He knew she was missing. Van was looking for her. It was almost like she could feel his urgency, or maybe she was just projecting it. Either way, it made her have courage.

An unknown amount of time ticked by and a door opened. More feet moved across the smooth floor.

"Well, what do we have here? A present for me?"

Cora froze. The universe was playing a colossal joke on her. It wasn't fair or reasonable for her to have to deal with this asshole again.

Fucking Chaz.

A gleeful Chaz ripped the fabric off her head. "Surprised to see me, babe?"

Cora looked around the room to find herself in something that looked like an office building. The room was plain, with bare white walls. One wall had windows that looked out over to the adjoining building. A desk and a chair in one corner and the chair she was sitting in were the only pieces of furniture in the room. Other than that, there were no clear clues to her location.

"No, I'm not. You're like a piece of dog shit that gets on your shoe. Even when you scrape it off, you can still smell it."

Chaz pulled back a hand and slapped her hard across the face. He'd never lifted a finger against her.

This was something different and dangerous from him.

"Oh, you don't like that? Feeling my hand on your face? Well guess what, I don't like being played for a fool!"

"A fool?" Cora laughed. She wasn't going to show any fear to this asshole. "Do you think I planned this?"

"Didn't you?"

"Oh yes, I had planned all along to get kidnapped by the people you owed money to! Then, I schemed for the man that *you* hired to rescue me, to be a Kindred that just happened to be looking for a mate. Wow, I'm good!"

That got her another slap. He was putting some heat behind it now. Like he'd been planning on hitting her.

"So what's your plan here, Chaz? Rape me? Kill me?"

"Killing you won't fix my problems," he said, rubbing his hands together. "And if you think I'd have you after that animal has touched you? No fucking way."

"Yes, *your* problems. Nothing I had anything to do with," she reminded him, trying not to let his comment about Van get under her skin. That was what he wanted. He wanted to hurt her.

"It doesn't matter. Did you know your new animal paid off all your debts? He just wire transferred the total amount to me."

Cora didn't know Van had done that. She hadn't asked him to do that, but she wasn't surprised either. She gritted her teeth and glared at him. "So you got what you wanted, what is this about?"

"This is about being bested by an animal! He stole you from me!" Chaz shouted, spittle flying from the edge of his mouth. His face was red and blotchy and he'd never looked so small to her as he did standing there.

Cora started laughing and shaking her head. "Seriously? This is about him being Kindred?"

"This is about you betraying your species!"

She couldn't believe it. The Dillard family had always been so careful when they spoke about the Kindred in public and even private. As if they knew that someone was always watching and listening, which they were. But the hatred and bigotry was deep-rooted and well hidden.

"My species? Listen to yourself. That's crazy talk," Cora said exasperatedly.

"Don't call me crazy!" Chaz screamed. "My mother warned me. She told me you weren't good enough for me, but I didn't listen. We had a good thing going. You didn't ask me about my business, and you let me do what I wanted as long as you had your apartment and your charity bullshit. Until you turned on me. I had enough shit coming down on me. I had problems. You didn't stop to think about what I was going through!"

"I always thought about you, Chaz. I thought about you before myself for years! And I've done that for too long. I'm *worth* the attention. I'm *worth* someone seeing me and hearing me and treating me as if I matter. I see now that you don't understand that. You're too selfish."

Cora chanced a look over to the men that grabbed her. They were big men, rough looking and infinitely more dangerous than Chaz. They lounged casually against the desk, looking bored with the whole situation.

"Okay, so what now?" Cora said in a tempered tone that she knew would piss him off.

"Now, your animal pays me. He pays me for what he stole from me!"

"He didn't steal shit. You might want to remember *I* left *you*. I was already gone when those goons found me." Cora addressed the two men in black in the corner. "You two, by the way, are *way* better at your job than the last guys who kidnapped me. Thumbs up."

One of the men grunted at her, but there was a

twinkle in his eye. He was just there because he was getting paid. He didn't give a shit about her, or Chaz. No loyalty among thieves.

Being cocky was buying her time and she'd continue to do it as long as she could. It was helping her and making Chaz angry, which she didn't give a shit about. He could hit her if he wanted. She was sure he'd run out of energy with his floppy weak arms before he could do any real damage.

"Shut your fucking mouth, bitch," Chaz barked.

"Fine, Chaz. What now?" she made her voice sound as bored as she could.

"He'll want you back. I know it, and I know he'll pay anything to get you."

"So it's back to money? You like to waste yours so you want someone else to pay your debts? That's very manly of you, good job."

Her head knocked back at the next crack of his hand against her cheek. That one definitely stung.

"I get my money and he can get whatever is left of you," Chaz sneered.

That didn't sound good to her at all.

CHAPTER 27

"**W**ell?"

Van was pacing in King's office. They had called all their contacts, looking for any scrap of information. Nothing had come back. It was as if she had disappeared entirely. They managed to run the plate of the SUV after their contact at SPD had run it for them. The vehicle was stolen, no surprise there.

After an hour, an email hit their main email account. It was a ransom demand. This time who ever sent it had bounced it through a number of servers making tracing it time consuming and it wasn't time they had.

The ransom was for two million dollars. Van didn't have two million dollars, but if he did, he'd be happy to hand it over for his mate's safe return. Whoever was asking knew that clans had access to more money than that. Clan Rekkr wouldn't even blink at that amount. If a member needed it, the Clan Head could give that money over. If it was for a good reason.

KSI often advised clients to pay ransom, if for no other reason but to get close to the criminals.

Van knew this wasn't a time to even pretend to pay the ransom. They had his mate and he wasn't going to give them any more time with her than they had already stolen from him.

King had offered up an option that didn't set well with him or Luca who had been stoically bringing up the rear like he was watching their backs as they focused on the task at hand.

Watching his boss's face, he knew that the furrowed brow and hard-set jaw meant he wasn't happy.

King dropped the phone, looked directly at Van and said, "They had eyes on him."

When King suggested calling the Kristanzi family, Van thought he'd lost his mind. But Luca had mentioned that if Chaz was in as deep a debt as this with the Kirstanzi family, then somebody would be keeping tabs on him.

"They were just about to go after him when I

called. They agreed to let us go in first. As long as we don't kill him."

Van didn't like that. He didn't know if he was going to be able to control himself when he came face to face with Charles Dillard III. He had been keeping in contact with Cora through their mark, but except for that one time, she hadn't answered back. That meant she couldn't. That meant they had done something to prevent her from reaching out to him.

"Why?" Van growled.

"They want him. Honestly, they can have him. I know you want to tear his throat out, but he owes them money and they'll make him suffer much more than your quick death would bring. Getting your mate back is our only priority."

Van wanted to argue, his animal side wanted to punish the man so bold as to touch what belonged to him.

"Fine, where are they?" It was going to take all of his control to not draw blood when he got there, but Cora was his primary target and he had to focus on the love that he felt for her. She didn't need to see him tearing a man apart.

His mate deserved a vacation, and as soon as he got her back in his arms, he was going to delay her introduction to the clan. Van was going to take her somewhere warm and tropical where she could recoup properly.

"Bellevue, they're in a medical office building that's being renovated. It's empty." King was picking his phone back up. "I'm calling everyone back. I want everyone on this."

"We should go now," Van growled.

"No, we need to go in prepared so there is no chance of Cora getting hurt."

Van growled, but he knew that King was right. He didn't have to like it, but he couldn't argue that Cora's safety came first.

As they geared up, each minute that passed tore at his heart. He found himself touching his mark as often as he could. He didn't want her to think for more than a minute that he wasn't coming for her.

Anson and Eden came rushing into the office from the previous job. They didn't even bother giving King a debrief. They knew that there was someone's life hanging in the balance. Details could wait.

Behind them came Zion, carrying a travel bag slung over his shoulder.

"Zion?" Van said surprised to see him.

"Got the message at the airport. I'm here, where do you want me?"

"At my back. Luca, I need you to have eyes if you

can," Van said, looking to their sharpshooter. Luca nodded as he packed up his rifle.

King spoke up to the others, "Anson, Eden, I want you two to cover all possible exits, move in once we've breached the floor. Kristanzi's man said that they are holed up on a third floor room. Luca can cover the entrance they're most likely to use. No one leaves that building on two feet."

Luca nodded. He knew that meant no casualties if he could help it, but it didn't mean he couldn't cause some damage.

Van gave Luca a hard look. Hopefully it translated to 'shoot whoever you want.' Luca gave him an evil smile, so Van had to assume he got the message.

The group continued to plan as they all grabbed their guns. This was one of those ops that could go a number of different ways.

Van didn't really care which way it went, as long as they got moving. Fast.

"Let's go, I want my mate back within the hour."

There were certain things you learned only by experience. Cora didn't think she was ignorant. She'd been around and she liked to learn new things. She was usually a whiz at Jeopardy, too.

Tonight, Cora learned something new. Being cut hurts. It hurts horribly. It is a continuous searing pain that you couldn't escape.

The blood was pouring down her cheeks, making her skin wet and warm.

It hurt. It hurt so much it took her breath away.

When Chaz brought out the knife she assumed he was just trying to scare her. He didn't have the balls to do anything with it. And that's exactly what she told him.

"You think you're so smart. You've got a big bear to be your own personal bodyguard. Well, where is he? He's not here, because you are just a human to him. He may be drawn to you, but he still has other things that come before you."

Chaz pointed the knife at her and used the tip to scrape against her shirt collar, dragging the fabric down to expose her mate mark. The tip of the knife left a shallow but stinging line of blood in its trail. The blade stopped at the edge of her mark.

"You little slut! Don't think I don't know what that means. You realize no real man will have you again. You've been branded by that animal!"

"I have, and I don't ever have to think about another man but him. I only want him, Chaz. He's strong and caring, and he loves me! Why would I ever settle for less... why would I ever settle for someone like you," she sneered.

"I wonder what would happen if I cut it off you..." he said thoughtfully.

"No!" Cora screamed before she could stop herself. She didn't want to give him an ounce of satisfaction that his torment was working.

"Don't worry, I know that would make me an enemy of the Kindred," he said, removing the knife.

"You think this won't? Kidnapping a mate?"

"No, I think that as long as he gets you back alive, he'll be happy. Besides, I made sure that my fingerprints are nowhere near this little adventure. It's all going to be pinned on anti-Kindred radicals."

Cora didn't think that any of that was plausible, but it showed how naïve Chaz really was. It wasn't her job to tell him that his plan was idiotic. It would be his downfall to experience.

On the plus side, Chaz said he was going to leave her alive. That meant all this bravado was just that. At least that was what she hoped.

"You know," Chaz said, tapping the flat of the knife against his chin. "I don't see why he doesn't need a reminder of who had you first."

Cora only saw the flash of light off the edge of the blade before the explosive pain raked across her face. She barely had time to gasp before Chaz's arm swung again, cutting her other cheek.

There had been a moment of shock, absolute horror as she realized what he had done. He'd cut her. Her face! She didn't know how deep or how big the cuts were, all she could focus on was the pain. Tears poured down her face as she whimpered and strained against her ropes.

"Not so cocky now, are we?" He'd said, tossing the knife casually onto the desk.

Cora didn't care now that he saw her crying. Her tears were mixing with the blood dripping down her face and off her jaw. The cruelty of what he'd done had shocked her just as much as the act itself. He'd scarred her, on purpose, just to hurt her and a man he barely knew. How could he go from being so indifferent to her, to having such rage? Had he been hiding this side of himself from her this entire time?

So many things flashed through her mind. What would Van think of her now? Her heart told her that he wouldn't care. He wasn't like that, and he'd already done so much for her that there was no way his actions were superficial.

Van would love her despite how she looked. It made her realize how much she loved him. He was there for her without question. He'd literally rescued her, not just from her kidnappers, but also from a miserable life. A life that was taking away any hope at happiness.

Van had swept in and offered up his heart and his life to her. She had to have faith in him that her future hadn't changed just because of what was happening to her in that moment.

One thing was for sure, no matter how this all ended, she needed to tell him that she loved him.

CHAPTER 28

Van and his team approached the building. It's was ten stories tall with a beige façade that looked like any other medical office building, except for the fact that it was surrounded by chain-link fences and construction equipment. Luca slipped away to set up a position to cover the door where the abandoned SUV was now sitting. Next to that SUV was a dusty, bright red Ferrari with a dented fender. That had to be Chaz's car. Van grimaced. Spending that much money on a car just to treat it like something they'd taken off a used car lot? Chaz Dillard was a douchebag of the highest order.

King had confirmed everyone's assignments while they were en route. He'd received a message while they'd been en route, and Van could feel his boss's tense vibe turn to pure rage.

"Van, I need you to fucking remember that if you shred my leather with your claws it's coming out of your pay. There's too many people in here for you to lose your focus!"

Van immediately went on alert. He started growling, unable to control his reaction.

King turned his phone towards him and the screen held one picture. It was of Cora, her face bloodied, her eyes closed, her tears making tracks through the blood.

Van roared, making the windows rattle. The other Kindred in the vehicle hunched at the anger he was venting. They knew how they would react if it was their mate in that photo.

"You need to keep your shit locked down until we get to her," King ordered.

"He fucking cut her!" Van felt like his heart was tearing out of his chest. She'd been hurt, on his watch, again. The first time he couldn't have done anything. This time he shouldn't have let her out of his sight. Not when she wasn't fully free of that scum.

"He'll pay. He'll wish he'd never been born. But Cora comes first. Take all that anger and focus it on finding her."

Van didn't know if he could. The hair on his body was sprouting and retracting as he tried to control his shift. His fangs were out and he didn't care, he would use them to tear Chaz's throat out.

"He's mine," Van growled.

"No shit," Luca said from the front seat.

When they arrived, the team broke off into their formations like a well-oiled machine. Van and King were taking lead; Anson and Eden disappeared around the side of the building, seeking a different exit. Zion followed King and Van, keeping a short distance so that no one could sneak up behind them.

Van was fighting his shift, his animal side wanted to be bigger and stronger, and most importantly, lethal.

He could only control it so far as they moved through the building. He knew his canines were showing and he had to plan how he was going to fire if needed because his claws had pushed out of his fingers, impeding his ability to use his gun. He tried to calm himself, but they weren't retracting.

King looked back at him and shook his head. Van wasn't going to shift, at least not yet. His human frame fit through doorways better than a hulking bear.

Taking the stairs between floors, they moved quickly and quietly. Van wanted to be in the lead, but he wasn't a hundred percent. His wounds were still healing so he had to put his desperation for his mate aside and allow King to take point.

Reaching the third floor, they both paused, using their extra sensitive hearing to decide if the door could be breached.

Nothing was on the other side, no movement, no breathing. Van opened the door slowly, grateful that the hinges made no sound. The hallway ahead of them was empty. Moving down it, they constantly scanned for threats. There were construction materials stacked in offices and common areas.

Taking a pause to get their bearings, King tapped his earpiece making it chirp in Van's ear. A second passed before Luca's voice came over the comms, "Third floor, twenty windows in, four people in the room. Two in black, one in a pink polo shirt and our target in a chair."

Van was happy to hear that Cora was in there. He wasn't happy that Luca hadn't commented on her condition. He didn't say anything on purpose. If Cora was safe, he would have said so.

Glancing back down the hallway, Van did a quick calculation of how far they had moved through the office building. The room Luca had specified should be just ahead. As they got closer to the door, they could hear Chaz Dillard's voice. And Van felt his hackles start to rise. Another male voice, low and brooding could be heard behind the door.

Van and King flanked the door, both listening and assessing before acting. Van wanted to bust the door down and get his mate. But he didn't know who had guns and who didn't. He couldn't risk her being in the line of fire.

Listening again, he heard the other voice talking. "The email has been sent. They have your ransom demand now. And the photos. All we have to do is wait."

"I know they fucking have the money. Everybody knows those animals are rich," Chaz responded.

"You better hope so. I heard you owe some people some money. How did you get yourself in that hole anyway?"

"Fucking horses. I've just had a run of bad luck. I'll get it all back, though. I don't need my father's money. They all think I can't make my own fortune. They'll see. I'll be a millionaire soon enough. Then I'm fucking out of here. I'm going to go south. Maybe Brazil, live large down there."

"Yeah, man, super idea," the other man said, not even hiding the derision in his voice.

Van looked at King and tried to gauge their next actions. King gave a small negative shake of his head, urging him to be patient. Grinding his teeth, Van waited.

There was movement inside the room.

"No reason for me to hang out here. My work is done," Chaz's sickening laugh came through the door. "You know to use my burner phone. Don't let this bitch out of your sight for any reason whatsoever. No bathroom breaks, nothing. I don't care if she pisses herself sitting there."

Van was feeling homicidal now. He glanced at King for confirmation, and his boss' eyes flashed yellow at him.

That was the sign he needed. Before shifting he ran his fingers over his mark one more time. It was a sign to Cora that he was coming for her. Holstering his gun and ripping off his vest, he kicked off his boots, and he pulled out his clan knife, using it to slice through his clothes and let his animal burst through his still aching flesh. He knew that if he went in low, they wouldn't be expecting him. King could bring up the rear high. Anyone that got past them would run into Zion. Too bad for them.

Van held his breath. His muscles were tensed as he crouched low; he dug his claws into the carpet outside the door. He could be fast when he wanted to. This was a moment for a burst of speed that would hopefully take everyone inside the room off guard.

"Call me when you hear something," Chaz ordered. The door handle started to move and Van braced himself.

The door pulled open and he heard King suck in a breath. As soon as the door was halfway open, they could see Chaz looking over his shoulder, smiling back at someone. It was also his first breath of his mate, and her blood. Van didn't wait. With a roar that shook the windows in the room beyond, Van lunged at the door, his shoulder knocking Chaz to the floor. The other man landed with an undignified grunt, and he began to shriek as he registered the fact that a giant bear was charging through the door.

King entered the room behind Van, firing over his shoulder as one of the thugs raised his gun. The man got a single round off that ricocheted off the door frame before King put a bullet into his shoulder, spinning him out of the chair and sending him crashing against the wall. A crash happened a second later as the middle window behind the desk shattered, glass exploding into the room.

The second man jerked and fell forward. A bloom of blood pooling on his upper shoulder, his hand still on the gun he had drawn.

Van bit down on Chaz's upper arm just enough

to puncture the skin and dragged him over to where Cora was tied to a chair.

"Please! Please don't kill me!" Chaz cried, tears pouring down his face. Van roared, inches from the pathetic man's face, showing him all of his teeth.

"Van?" Cora's voice was full of awe and relief. Van looked over to his mate, he knew she was alive because he could feel her heartbeat just as strongly he could feel his own.

When he saw her, he let out a cry that was half roar, half cry. His mate was covered in blood. There were open wounds on both of her cheeks. The cuts were deep, blood had poured down her cheeks and stained her clothing.

"Van, is that you?"

She looked so relieved, that he made a chuffing noise at her. He wasn't going to let the piece of shit off the floor. Not yet.

Turning his head back to focus on Chaz, pinned to the floor underneath his massive paw, he growled low, letting his hot breath cover the man's face. Chaz recoiled and Van hated him even more.

"It wasn't me! They did it. I didn't do it," Chaz lied.

Van knew it wasn't the other men, even though the one conscious one protested from the floor. "Fuck you, asshole!" The second man lay quiet on the floor. King had only winged him in the arm but he had fainted right after.

Cora gave him a look that told him she was happy to see him, but smiling wasn't an option. He saw red, not just from the blood on her face, but the rage within that was clouding his vision.

"Don't bother killing him, Van. He's not worth it," Cora whispered.

Van didn't agree. Killing him was definitely worth it. He would be totally justified with ending the life of such a waste of space.

"Van," he heard again. It wasn't that she didn't want him dead. It was that she didn't want Van to be the one to do it. He understood that. Van brought his muzzle as close to Chaz's face as he could. Chaz had turned his head as he cried.

Out of the corner of his eye, Van saw Zion and Anson rushing in to secure the other two men. Eden was behind Cora, untying her.

It was possible that they could finish this and move on. But Chaz deserved more than a free ride to jail.

King spoke up, "I made a deal with the Kristanzis, Van. I'm not going to earn an enemy by not handing him over."

That was all Van needed to hear. Whipping his four-inch claws over Chaz's face, his claws ripped into the man's skin, giving him matching cuts so he could remember what he'd done to Cora. Even if he survived his debt repayment plan, no plastic surgeon would ever make him look like he did before.

Chaz screamed and continued to scream until Van roared at him, stifling the man's yell down to a whimper. Zion pulled Chaz out from under Van, which was probably a good idea. Seeing that piece of shit bleed satisfied the animal that he was.

Once Zion had Chaz under control and was cuffing him, Van let his body shift back, pushing his animal back now that the danger was contained. His shift had hurt, and his body was resisting, the adrenaline still pumping through his muscles. He stood just as Eden had finished untying Cora and his mate flew into his arms, her forehead resting against his naked chest.

It wasn't close enough, but he didn't want to hurt her face. "Baby, I'm so sorry," Van said, squeezing her and kissing the top of her head.

"It's not your fault. I shouldn't have left. I was stupid," she cried.

Eden stepped forward, apologizing briefly as she pressed a square of clean gauze against Cora's face. He heard her gasp and his heart twisted in his chest.

"Van, let us help her. Anson has clothes," King said quietly but firmly.

Van didn't want to let her go. He never wanted to let her go ever again. But she needed care.

"I've got her," King assured him.

With a barely audible grumble, Van released her, and King pulled Cora into his arms as Eden tried to stem the flow of blood. Normally Van wouldn't have let anyone touch his mate. But King wasn't holding her like a lover. His arms were offering temporary support. He could see that Cora was shaking, and he was grateful to his friend.

"I'll call Dr. Liz on the way. Do you want her to come to the office or your place?" King asked.

Van pulled on a pair of pants and a shirt before taking Cora back into his embrace. "My place."

"Dr. Liz?" Cora asked.

"She'll stitch up your face," he said softly.

"Oh, Van, I'm so sorry. I'm going to look like a freak!" she cried.

"Hush, don't worry about that now."

Chaz was glaring at Cora, and Van growled in his throat. "Call the Kristanzis, arrange to drop that piece of shit off."

"No! No, I'll make you a deal. They'll kill me if you hand me over!" Chaz pleaded.

"You are gonna wish they killed you," Luca said softly, smiling coldly at the human in front of him. "They'll just slice off pieces of you and mail them to your father until he pays up. You'd better hope that he isn't into collecting too many pieces before he gives in."

Chaz let out a pitiful scream before he was dragged out of the room.

Van turned to King, "The other two?"

"I can tell just by looking at them that the SPD is looking for them. They don't look like upstanding individuals, do they? I'll have Zion and Luca handle it. We'll drive you back to your place."

Bending down, Van picked Cora up into his arms. She rested her face against his heart cushioned by a layer of fabric and gauze.

They took the elevators down this time and Van tucked Cora in the back seat before getting in. He pulled her back into his lap and she didn't protest. Her body was limp and exhausted against his.

He'd failed her. He should have done more. It was going to be a long time before he forgave himself. More importantly, he needed Cora to trust that he could protect her. But those conversations could wait. He had her back in his arms. She was breathing and that was enough.

"Van?" she whispered, tipping her head back up to him.

"Yeah, sweets?"

"I'm glad he didn't kill me," she said.

Van sucked in his breath. It was agony to hear her saying the words he'd been thinking the whole time he was apart from her.

"I wouldn't have let him," Van said roughly. It was a promise that he could easily have failed to fulfill.

"I mean, I'm glad. Because I didn't want to die without telling you that I love you. I do, Van. I love you so much," she said, her eyes full of tears. Cora brought her hand up to her mate mark and placed her whole palm over it.

Van felt the heat and connection spread through him, and the sensation made him gasp. "I love you, Cora. More than anything in the world."

Cora smiled, her lips barely moving because of her wounds. But he could see it. It was all in her eyes.

CHAPTER 29

Cora squeezed Van's hand as Dr. Liz placed more lidocaine into her cheek. She'd already stitched one side closed and was now on the other side.

When they had arrived at Van's loft, he'd placed her on the bed and helped her change out of her bloodstained clothes. He'd gently wiped off as much of the blood on her jaw and chest as he could before the doctor showed up.

Dr. Liz was a middle-aged woman with silver reflective eyes. She was friendly and clucked her tongue in a matronly way at the state of Cora's face.

Her eyes distracted Cora and Dr. Liz laughed. "I'm a snow leopard, sweetie. Sleek and beautiful.

Not like these big smelly bears," she said with a wink.

Cora would have loved to see her animal, but asking would be considered rude.

"Shouldn't I see a plastic surgeon? I'm not really vain, but still," Cora asked.

She didn't want to end up a scarred mess. Van might still love her, but she didn't want to go through life being stared at. Maybe she was a little vain.

Dr. Liz pulled down the neck of her shirt, exposing her mate mark. "I'm thinking you're going to heal up just fine."

Van squeezed her hand and she turned her gaze to him. "It'll be okay."

Cora wanted to believe him, so she nodded. Dr. Liz finished up with her suture and gave Cora a shot that made her feel woozy, but the pain in her face faded to a warm sensation even after the lidocaine wore off.

Dr. Liz promised to visit in a few days to check in on her and remove the stitches, and then she left them alone. Cora knew that was what Van wanted, and she wanted it too. Cora was cuddled into a warm strong chest as she floated on a haze of medication. "Shouldn't my stitches be in longer?" she asked Van.

"You seem to be forgetting, sweets, you're part Kindred now."

Cora frowned. "So?"

"It means I can help you along in the healing process."

"But how?"

"Get some sleep. Right now, your body needs to heal. We'll talk about that later." Cora wanted to argue with him, but the medicine was making her feel lovely and she didn't want to keep fighting it. She drifted off, hoping there wouldn't be any bad dreams waiting for her.

***

Waking to a dark room, Cora felt something wet against her cheek and thought her stitches had opened and she was bleeding again.

Then she felt something soft and rough at the same time swipe across her cheek. Focusing through the darkness she saw Van leaning over her.

"Did you just lick me?" she asked, horrified.

"Yes."

"But, why?" she sputtered.

"Because I'm helping you. It will make your wounds heal faster."

"Seriously? Licking them? That can't be sanitary."

"You don't complain when I lick your pussy," he said, his voice sounding amused.

"Totally different situation and you know it!" she said aghast.

"Sweets, if I can heal your face, then I can fuck you. And trust me, I really need to fuck you so I can get that asshole's scent off you."

"A shower would do the trick there," she said.

"No, he etched himself into you, your fear of him left you vulnerable. No shower will wash that away. I need you to be mine, wear my scent, be claimed by me alone."

Cora reached up to touch his rough bearded cheek. "I am yours, no matter what I smell like. This," she said, touching her mark. "Makes us forever. Nobody can ever break that."

"You're right, but it will still make me feel better," he said, growling low.

"Fine, lick away. I could use an orgasm myself," she said, not believing she was uttering those words. Life with Van was going to be full of surprises she was sure.

CHAPTER 30

The champagne cork flew across the room as Ida yelped at the noise.

Ethel ducked as the cork flew past her. "Why must you always make a big production of it? You know you can just twist those off. No fuss, no muss, and no mess!"

"I love when we can all get together," Ida declared. "We need champagne!" Ida started to pour into the glasses each Crone held.

"I'm not saying we don't, and you act like we never see each other," Ethel tsked. "We have more frequent flier miles than most business executives."

"I love those warm cookies in first class," Mary said wistfully.

"Oh, those are good. I always sneak a few extra when I use the lavatory," Fannie admitted.

"I'm really hoping it's after you use the facilities and you aren't in there crunching away on the toilet," Velma said with a wide-eyed look.

The six Crones were sitting in the library of the Head of Clan Rekkr's home. They had all gathered to witness the presentation of Van's new mate. It was a joyous event that needed to be celebrated. No matter how many times they had done it before, it was always a thrill to welcome a new mate.

"You know, she's already carrying," Ida said, her eyes twinkling.

"Are you sure?" Velma asked, holding out her glass for a refill.

Ida stopped and eyeballed Velma's glass knowing good and well that she'd just filled it. "Of course I'm sure. I had a dream last night of a beehive and a field of lilies."

"And that means she's expecting?" Ruth asked.

"Of course, what else could it possibly mean?" Ida said annoyed. "Clearly the bees are fertility, you know because of the honey, and the lilies, well it's going to be a girl."

"Oh pish, you think you're so clever," Mary said shaking her head.

"We'll just see, won't we?" Ida said gleefully. She

felt what the dream meant more than she knew for certain. It felt right and she knew that questioning the Great Mother often led to her messing things up.

"They do make a beautiful couple. Makes me miss my Henry," Betty said with a smile.

"It's not like he's gone, Betty. Those fools are just up at the cabin fishing and you know they aren't catching anything!" Ruth scoffed.

"That's because they're drinking, not fishing," Mary sighed.

"Let them have their fun. It keeps them out of our hair. They know what they got saddled with and the Great Mother has rewarded them with beautiful, clever mates," Ida said, fluffing her curly white hair.

"True, true, they are lucky bastards," Fannie said raising her glass. "To the men, they think they have won the prize but are too adorably dim to realize that Frigga has a hilarious sense of humor!"

"To the men!"

EPILOGUE

V an picked up two glasses of champagne as a waiter walked by. He was standing in the grand entry talking to King. Or, listening at least. His eyes kept creeping to the top of the stairs waiting to catch a glimpse of her.

Lost in thought he felt a heavy hand land on his shoulder.

"Thanks for the invite," Anson said, taking the glass out of Van's hand. "How'd you swing it anyway? I'm a Fehu infiltrating the Rekkr."

Van took his glass back. "Get your own. I told Elias you were providing additional security."

"You lied?" King said in surprise.

"No, Anson is always on. Besides he is seeing

everything with fresh eyes. I don't think there will be any issues with Cora's ex."

Anson snorted. "Didn't you hear?"

Van frowned. "No, what?" his gaze went between the men.

King cleared his throat, "I figured it was something we could talk about later."

"Seems serious," Van said bracing himself.

"Not really," Anson said, a wicked smirk on his face. "You're mate's ex is safely back home in the loving arms of his family."

"How'd that happen?" Van really hoped that he'd never be heard from again. He was counting on it.

"Oh, not to worry. It took two fingers and an ear before his daddy paid up."

"Fuck," Van hissed. He didn't like that asshole. In fact, he hated him. Van had already left him scarred for life. The Kristanzis had made sure that nobody would ever look at him the same way ever again.

"I'm kind of surprised it took that much to get his father to pay up. He really took his time weighing out his options," King said shaking his head.

"As long as I never see him again, and my mate never has to think about him again, I'm fine with that."

King nodded. "Agreed. Actually, Anson, I've got a job for you when you get back."

"Can't Hudson do it?" Anson asked. "I was going to go find some rocks to climb. No ropes, just me and nature."

"Hudson got a lead so he won't be back for a while. But I have a stalker case for you," King said taking a drink.

"A real one? This isn't a groupie is it? You know, I don't think that shit is funny when you get me to talk to them."

Van laughed at that. They had set Anson up with a groupie a few times. He was gullible.

"Legitimate. Years of harassment. I know you like puzzles. It will be good for you," King said.

Anson let out a low growl and Van looked up the stairs again for his mate.

Cora twirled in her silver sequined gown. This was a gown that beat the ruined wedding dress she'd been wearing when she met Van by miles. The bodice was low cut with the rest of the dress hugging her curves in a gentle but seductive way before it flared out in a mermaid tail full of ruffles. One strap held the dress up over her shoulder with the other side strapless, revealing her mate mark. She felt beautiful, happy, and best of all, there was someone there to appreciate all of it.

"I'm so glad I still have a little color. I think being mated has finally kept me from burning to a crisp!" she said to her mother who was helping her fix a silver rose into her hair.

"Two weeks on a beach, you're one lucky lady," Molly said, eyes smiling at her daughter.

"It was just what I needed." Cora leaned closer to the full-length mirror. She was wearing her red hair down in big bouncy waves. One side pinned up with the rose. She rubbed her red lips together, smoothing her lipstick. Her eyes flashed over her cheeks to the pencil white lines that weren't even visible under her foundation.

Van's unorthodox home treatment had done the trick. Dr. Liz was able to remove her stitches after two days, by the time they were ready to leave for the Caribbean her wounds had healed to the barely noticeable faint scars they were now.

Cora had been happily laid out on the beach at a private Kindred only club that was owned by a local clan. The drinks flowed freely and she never wanted to leave. Van made love to her every chance he got. She knew he loved her and he found her sexy. Still there was a focus that she found adorable. He wanted children; she could see it in his eyes. After her experience, she was completely on board. She wanted his baby, and wanted to build their family as soon as possible.

Now they were in the southeast corner of Oregon, the heart of Clan Rekkr and the home of the Clan Head, preparing for her to be introduced as Van's mate.

Cora and Van had flown in, meeting up with Cora's parents so that everyone could be there. Van's parents were wonderful and gushed over her. She met his sister Nicole and her family. Nicole's ridiculously hysterical sons treated Van like a jungle gym and Cora could tell that he was a well-loved uncle. Van adored those boys and it made Cora want to give him a child even more.

The ceremony to announce her as mate was a little debutante-ish, regardless of the gender of the mate. The clan gathered, at least all that could come. These were 'everyone welcome' events, so most made their best efforts to be there.

It had all been explained, and Cora was ready. At least, she thought she was ready. The Clan Head, in this case Elias, would announce that Van had found his mate and had claimed her as his own. After that, the Clan was to accept her and welcome her as one of their own. It was formal, but very sweet.

She was then supposed to walk down a long curving staircase with hundreds of eyes on her. When she reached the bottom she would make an oath accepting her place in the clan, promising to keep all its secrets, and to never forsake their bond.

Cora hadn't told her parents yet that she and Van had gotten married in a private ceremony on that Caribbean beach. It was something she needed to confirm her human bond with him. He'd happily agreed and they had exchanged vows at sunset. It had been beautiful.

Cora looked at her mom who was positively beaming at her. "I'm ready," Cora said confidently. Her man was waiting for her at the bottom of the stairs, and she hadn't seen in him in a few hours. After she made her oath tonight, she would tell him about the little life she knew that she carried inside her. She'd wait for the moment when he looked the happiest and whisper it into his ear.

"No butterflies?" her mom asked.

"No, this runaway bride is running straight into the arms of the man she loves."

CONNECT WITH MOXIE

Thank you so much for reading my story. There are more to come so be sure to sign up for my Newsletter or follow me on Facebook and Twitter.

Subscribe to newsletter at:
moxienorth.net/newsletter
New Releases, Giveaways, and Shenanigans

facebook.com/moxienorthbooks
twitter.com/moxienorthbooks

facebook.com/moxienorthbooks

twitter.com/moxienorthbooks

instagram.com/moxienorth

amazon.com/authors/moxienorth

pinterest.com/moxienorth

PACIFIC NORTHWEST BEARS

Be My Bear

Bearly Cooking

Bear in Mind

Bear With Me

Bearly Healed

Bearly a Memory

Bearly Breathing

Angel: Rochon Bears

Rainier: Rochon Bears

Finely: Rochon Bears

PACIFIC NORTHWEST COUGARS

Cougar's Victory

Cougar's Luck

Cougar's Gift

REDEMPTION MC

Wounded Wolf

7 BRIDES FOR 7 BEARS

Runaway Bride

Willing Bride (March 2018)

SOUTHERN SHIFTERS KINDLE WORLD

Stick Shifter

Rough Edges

ONE TRUE MATE KINDLE WORLD

Bear's Embrace

NOVELLAS

Jingle Bears

Valentine's Surprise

Made in the USA
Lexington, KY
28 February 2019